FAEDOM

Written by Agnes Monod-Gayraud
and Lorna White
Illustrated by Nadzeya Makeyeva

*Dedicated to Fred, Charlotte, Scarlett and Sylvia...
and all the big and little fairies in our lives* – A.M.G. & L.W.

Dedicated to my beloved parents – Tatsiana & Uladzimir – N.M.

BIG PICTURE PRESS

FIRST PUBLISHED IN THE UK IN 2024 BY BIG PICTURE PRESS,
AN IMPRINT OF BONNIER BOOKS UK,
4TH FLOOR, VICTORIA HOUSE,
BLOOMSBURY SQUARE, LONDON, WC1B 4DA
OWNED BY BONNIER BOOKS
SVEAVÄGEN 56, STOCKHOLM, SWEDEN
WWW.BONNIERBOOKS.CO.UK

TEXT COPYRIGHT © 2024 BY AGNES MONOD-GAYRAUD
AND LORNA WHITE
ILLUSTRATION COPYRIGHT © 2024 BY NADZEYA MAKEYEVA
SOME ILLUSTRATIONS PROVIDED BY MUTI
DESIGN COPYRIGHT © 2024 BY BIG PICTURE PRESS

1 3 5 7 9 10 8 6 4 2

ALL RIGHTS RESERVED

ISBN 978-1-80078-495-6

THIS BOOK WAS TYPESET IN ROYLLES, TYPHONE
AND BASKERVILLE.
THE ILLUSTRATIONS WERE CREATED
AND COLOURED DIGITALLY.

EDITED BY JOANNA MCINERNEY, MATT RALPHS
AND EMILY THOMAS
DESIGNED BY NATHALIE EYRAUD,
JENNY HASTINGS AND MELISSA MCINERNEY
PRODUCTION BY CHÉ CREASEY

PRINTED IN CHINA

FAEDOM

Enter the Fairy Realm

AGNES MONOD-GAYRAUD & LORNA WHITE
ILLUSTRATED BY NADZEYA MAKEYEVA

BPP

CONTENTS

WELCOME TO FAEDOM 10

FAIRIES AND FAUNA 12

EARTH FAIRIES 15

INTRODUCTION TO EARTH FAIRIES 17

ROWAN: *The Tree Fairy* 18

ROSIE, PEONY & AZALEA: *The Flower Fairies* 20

ESMERALDA: *The Moss & Meadow Fairy* 22

NIAH: *The Cave Fairy* 24

SORELLA: *The Mouse Fairy* 26

LUNELLA: *The Moon Fairy* 28

LUNELLLA'S GUIDE TO THE MOON 30

WATER FAIRIES 33

INTRODUCTION TO WATER FAIRIES 35

MARINA: *The Oceans & Seas Fairy* 36

NEPHELIE: *The Mist & Steam Fairy* 38

ONDINE: *The Rivers & Lakes Fairy* 40

ISA: *The Snow & Ice Fairy* 42

TALIA: *The Rain & Dew Fairy* 44

SKYLAR: *The Rainbow Fairy* 46

ANATOMY OF FAIRY WINGS 48

FIRE FAIRIES 51

INTRODUCTION TO FIRE FAIRIES 53

SOLANGE: *The Sun Fairy* 54

SERAPHINA: *The Lava Fairy* 56

FARAH: *The Desert Fairy* 58

ALMA: *The Kitchen Fairy* 60

AKARI: *The Neon Fairy* 62

ASTER: *The Star Fairy* 64

LIFE CYCLE OF A STAR 66

AIR FAIRIES 69

INTRODUCTION TO AIR FAIRIES 71

WILHELMINA & GAIL:
The Wind & Storm Fairies 72

LIRAZ: *The Vanishing Fairy* 74

JAY: *The Bird Fairy* 76

SHAYAN & SHA'IRA:
The Song & Poetry Fairies 78

CELESTE: *The Dream Fairy* 80

JAZELLE: *The Shapeshifter Fairy* 82

FAIRY SPOTTING MAP 86

FEASTS AND FAE DAYS 88

FAEOLOGY CHARTS 90

**ABOUT THE AUTHORS
AND ILLUSTRATOR** 92

WELCOME TO FAEDOM

Fairies are the heart and soul of the enchanted world of the fae. They share this enigmatic realm with a panoply of mythical beings and beasts. Fantastic and familiar, they inhabit the woods, meadows and streams of all the fairy tales we have come to love through the ages.

ELVES

Elves are a supernatural race of immortal beings. They may be small in stature, but they have enormous magical powers. First mentioned in Germanic mythology, their legends have passed into Scandinavian, Celtic and English lore. In modern times, Tolkien's *Lord of the Rings* saga popularised the elvish tradition. Today's elves are best known for their efforts in making Christmas a magical season for humans, especially children.

DWARVES & GNOMES

Both dwarves and gnomes are small, human-like creatures with magical powers who prefer to dwell in forest burrows. They have been celebrated for their dedication to protecting Snow White from her evil stepmother, but they aren't always as forthcoming when it comes to human interactions. Their main purpose is to safeguard their buried treasure from greedy human hands.

MERFOLK, SELKIES & KELPIES

Close companions of the fairies of the oceans and seas, these aquatic creatures have populated many myths centred around the treacherous powers of the watery realm. Most often, they have been known to charm naïve sailors with their heavenly voices and beauty, dragging them down to their deaths at the bottom of the sea.

THE WITCHERY

The witches, wizards and magicians of this world live between the fae and earthly realms, weaving a hybrid magic that draws upon the rare resources and ancient wisdom hidden throughout the Cosmos.

FAE KNIGHTS

They are the original guardians of Faedom. Their main task is to keep humans out of the realm. Armed with incredible strength and possessing the heart of a lion, any knight of this order will stop at nothing to protect Faedom from earthly interference, slaying giants, dragons and evil kings in their wake.

GIANTS & OGRES

As gargantuan figures that have struck fear into the hearts of children over millennia, they have a rather grisly reputation. However, they aren't always so terrible and there are quite a few giants and ogres in Faedom who are as kind and generous as can be.

FAUNS & CENTAURS

These mythical creatures possess the torso and head of a human, but the lower body parts and legs of a goat or horse. They have appeared in thousands of legends throughout the centuries as both liberators and antagonists. Fauns play instruments and never miss a party, while the more serious centaurs will fiercely guard their territory to protect their loved ones from encroaching beasts and monsters.

FAE BESTIARY

Faedom would be a truly desolate place without its magical menagerie of mythical beasts, from the legendary unicorn and the resilient phoenix to the fearsome dragons, griffins, basilisks and sphinxes that eternally guard the best-kept secrets of this magical realm.

FAIRIES...

Fairies were born of the spark that illuminated the darkness as the Universe came into being many billions of years ago. They are the ancient fates, destinies, guardians, guides, gatekeepers, muses and messengers who have forged a bridge between the enchanted realm of magic and mysticism and the material world of nature and human civilisation.

These mystical heroes have been at the centre of epic mythologies, passed through the oral traditions of folk cultures across the globe over countless generations. The earliest written records of fairies include Ferdowsi's epic poem *Shahnameh* at the turn of the tenth century and the numerous fae that feature in medieval iterations of the Arthurian legends, to Shakespeare's own dramatic ode to the fae in *A Midsummer Night's Dream* four hundred years ago. And of course, there are the fairy tales that have been immortalised by countless retellings, the most famous of which were set down on paper by the Brothers Grimm and Hans Christian Andersen. Even Oscar Wilde compiled his own collection of charismatic fairy stories. Fairy tales have left an indelible mark on our world, transporting us to a place of imagination and wonder, while lending a vital lesson on human foibles and follies.

As charismatic and ageless as the Earth itself, the fae are our most valiant guardians and protectors, stopping at nothing to punish those who pollute and pillage our wonderful planet. Fairies have long been known for their mischief, conjuring up unusual circumstances and even sudden misfortunes to trip up their human neighbours. Their magic has piqued our curiosity through the ages, leading many astray in futile attempts to solve impossible mysteries or loot hidden fairy treasures. In a more trivial sense, fairies are often the ones to blame when household items go missing, or a recipe inexplicably goes wrong.

They are the Sprites, Pixies, Sidhe, Sith, Brownies, Greencoaties, Yarthkins, Spunkies, Spriggans, Tylwyth Teg, Rusalkas, Sylphs, Selkies and Nymphs of European legend. They are the Mazikeen of Jewish tradition and the Feu follet of Cajun beliefs. They are the Miru of Maori legend and the Menehune of Hawai'i. They are the Nûññë'hï of the Cherokee, Jogah of the Iroquois, the Alux of the Mayas and Chaneques of Mexico. They are the Vættir of Norway, the Encantado of Portugal, the Kashyali of the Roma, the Peri of Persia, the Hu Hsien of China, the Aziza of the Dahomey mythology of West Africa and they are close kin of the mystical Djinn of Asia.

...AND FAUNA

The Fairies of Faedom belong to an ancient order known as the Elementals: Earth, Water, Fire and Air. From the iridescent glint of a waterfall and the mysterious allure of the forest, to the divine melody of a song, they are the incarnation of natural, earthly spirits – plant, animal, even human, and everything in between. Yet those who are familiar with their mercurial ways will know that they would vehemently refuse to be so neatly boxed into categories. After all, the Moon Fairy's magic may be bound to the Earth, but the tidal pull she leans into links her to the sea. The Neon Fairy might glow as bright as a star, but the airiness of her spirit is what fuels her glamour and light. And while these mysterious beings may appear to be made of flesh and blood, unlike mortals, some of the fae can live forever and hold powers that go beyond the limits of the natural world. Like the elements, fairies hold the power to create and to destroy.

Trooping fairies wander about the Earth in boisterous cavalcades of merriment, but some are quite solitary and prefer to dwell alone. No matter their type, most fairies will make themselves scarce at the sight of a human. They will make an exception for children, especially those who have shown themselves to be kind, pure of heart and respectful of the natural order of things. Fairies will even go out of their way to protect a child who has been hurt or lost in the wilderness, often risking their own safety for the life of a small human.

To spot a fairy, you must prove your good intentions and find a portal between the earthly realm and the world of the fae, either through space or through time. There are many magical entrances to Faedom but the most common ones can be found in the hollow of a tree or a glowing fairy ring. Picking the right time is crucial. Portals will appear at the hinges of the day, month or year – such as dawn or dusk, the full moon, the equinox or the solstices. These are the liminal spaces where the veil between the spirit and material worlds momentarily disappears, giving us a glimpse at the scintillating forces behind the wonders of the natural world.

Welcome to the mystical realm of Faedom.

EARTH FAIRIES

ROWAN: THE TREE FAIRY

ROSIE, PEONY & AZALEA: THE FLOWER FAIRIES

ESMERALDA: THE MOSS & MEADOW FAIRY

NIAH: THE CAVE FAIRY

SORELLA: THE MOUSE FAIRY

LUNELLA: THE MOON FAIRY

EARTH FAIRIES

Born of ancient rock and soil, the Earth fairies are grounded and tenacious. Their spirits are as resolute as the trees and as delicate as the petals of a rose. Their roots are deeply anchored to the ancient history of the Cosmos, setting the rare foundations for life in the vastness of our Solar System. These fairies are the original architects of the world, sculpting the rugged landscapes of our planet into the cliffs, caves and coves that we have come to love so well. They bring about abundance, cultivating the ground and unearthing the riches of our planet. Their natural harmony strives to protect and nurture the treasures of this world, fighting a magical war against the greedy few who aim to pillage the Earth's sacred legacy.

THE TREE FAIRY

ROWAN

Rowan is a gentle giantess who towers over many of the smaller fae in her kingdom. She is a pillar of immeasurable strength and intelligence who embodies the natural order and magic spirit of the forest, captivating everyone who enters its bounds.

Though she is by far the most ancient forest spirit, Rowan's true age remains a secret. Every few thousand years, she perishes and is swiftly renewed, to reign over her tree kingdom once more. Her infinite arms stretch up to the sky, beckoning the clouds to share their rain with the forest. Rowan's long, twisted locks of hair change from green to gold with the seasons, crowned with a swirling ring of leaves. This crown joins with those of all the elders in her community, creating a royal canopy that provides shade for the creatures of the forest floor, allowing just enough sunlight to trickle in to feed the younger trees.

As the mother of the forest, Rowan provides shelter to all its creatures, big and small. She nurtures those who are hungry with fruits, leaves, seeds, nuts, sap, maple syrup, birch juice and mushrooms. She offers sanctuary to anyone running from danger – yet she will set traps for all villains who dare to invade her sacred forest. She guards the enchanted hollows of the wood that serve as portals between the human world and the fairy realm, making sure that no one can cross over and endanger the existence of the fae.

Like most fairies, Rowan is wary of humans and their intentions, but she does have a special fondness for children, helping them to climb her branches and catching them before they fall. Any child who feels anxious or unwell can place their hands upon the rough bark of any tree in the forest to feel her strength and support, and her mere presence has the power to raise the spirit. In truth, humans could not live without her life-giving breath of oxygen or her sustainable gifts of food, shelter and warmth.

Wondrous Wands

The wood of the rowan and other tree species is believed to have magical properties. If you come across a nice stick, pick it up and offer thanks to its tree. Bring it home, then decorate it with leaves and ribbons to create your own wondrous wand. Draw the Tree Fairy's symbol on a piece of paper and wrap it around the bottom of the stick. Inscribe her nurturing energy by chanting:

Forest spirit, we call on your powers to protect us and bring us joy!

TREE OF LIFE
Trees are sacred in various religions and mythologies, including the Bible's Tree of Life and Buddha's Bodhi tree. In Ancient Greece, dryads represented tree spirits, and worldwide, the spirits have diverse names, such as Thailand's Nang Tani, Madagascar's Rakapila and Lithuania's Lauma.

NATURAL NETWORKS
Scientists have found that trees are connected by a mycorrhizal network of roots and fungi that allows for the transfer of water and nutrients between them. This evolutionary feature ensures that each sapling has a maximum chance of surviving to adulthood, even with limited access to resources. Trees can be 'fed' through this 'wood wide web'.

FOREST BATHING
In Japan, the wellness practice Shinrin-yoku, or 'forest bathing', involves inhaling chemicals called phytoncides, released by trees during woodland walks. Researchers have found this can enhance mood, creativity and even physical health, including reducing blood pressure and boosting the immune system.

EARTH FAIRIES

ROSIE PEONY & AZALEA

FLORA & FAUNA

Insects and flowering plants have developed together over millennia in a process known as co-evolution. The bright colours and intense fragrances that characterise many species of flowers evolved to attract tiny pollinators who assist in transporting their seeds in exchange for a nutritious helping of nectar. Various species of birds and even bats also engage in this tasty trade-off.

CHARMING BOUQUETS

Throughout history, flowers have been associated with emotions and intentions. In Victorian England, roses depicted love, while lilies were meant to represent purity. The act of giving someone flowers signified a meaningful social interaction, or a symbol of affection, romance or sympathy, depending on the flower or bouquet. Even today, giving flowers as a gift remains a special gesture.

FLOWER FACE

The Welsh legend of Blodeuwedd tells the story of an enchanted woman created from the flowers of broom, meadowsweet and the oak tree by the magicians Math and Gwydion. Her name is a combination of the Welsh words blodau (flowers) and gwedd (face). When she betrays her husband and tries to have him killed, she is turned into an owl by the magicians as punishment and banished from appearing in the daytime.

THE FLOWER FAIRIES

The Flower Fairies are the world's tiniest and most devoted gardeners, cultivating every seedling until it blooms in a sudden burst of soft petals. They work closely with the birds, bees, butterflies and insects of the Earth to help fill the world with a dynamic spectrum of colours and scents. In exchange, they offer their little friends nourishing meals of nectar and pollen.

For these vibrant beings, there is no such thing as too much colour. They joyfully embellish Earth's rocky landscape with every possible hue, from the softest pink, lilac, yellow and white to bold fuchsia, crimson, deep purple and velvety black. In spring they cover the forest floor with a thick carpet of wildflowers, climbing to the very tops of the trees to sprinkle branches with lush clusters of fragrant blossoms.

While certain flowers and their fairies are shy, such as Buttercup and Petunia, others such as Orchid, Poppy and Peony are overwhelmingly expressive and dramatic. Some Flower Fairies prefer to come out in the dark, such as the Queen of the Night, dancing beneath the stars and basking in the moonlight. At dawn, these nocturnal fae wrap themselves up in their silken petals as birdsong lulls them to sleep, while Daisy and Morning Glory rise to the sky as the early Sun's rays light up the world.

There is nothing Flower Fairies enjoy more than a garden party, when they can don their prettiest dresses and most flamboyant hats, celebrating their natural beauty with boisterous bouts of singing and dancing. Their steps trace out fairy rings through fields and forests, forging a botanical link between the fae and earthly realms.

There are thousands of Flower Fairies inhabiting every sun-dappled island and continent known to humankind. Always out and about, these fairies are easy for humans to spot, but will vanish in a flash of colour and intoxicating scent. Legend has it that they may even leave behind some fairy treasure for children to find in a cluster of cowslips.

Flower Power

Take a walk through a nearby park or garden and whisper a wish to the Flower Fairies to win their favour and boost your day…

*Roses and jasmine for friendship and love,
A posy of peonies for a lucky penny,
Irises for wisdom and hydrangeas for energy,
Azaleas for elegance and poise,
Lavender for a restful night's sleep.*

Remember to thank the fairy for listening to your wish.

EARTH FAIRIES

THE MOSS & MEADOW FAIRY

ESMERALDA

Keeper and guardian of all things green, Esmeralda sweeps through wild prairies and grasslands, over insects and butterflies, whispering tales of enchanted locations hidden among the forests and babbling brooks of the countryside.

The Flower Fairies are her closest cousins and while Esmeralda admires their colourful creations, she has a single pragmatic purpose – to keep the Earth healthy and green. She does it by nourishing the grasses and wildflowers of pastures and fields, and feeding the creatures that live in the meadow, including the sweet cows, sheep and goats who spend their days grazing. She also recycles the Earth's green spaces, diligently attending to the vastest plains and the humblest patches of grass in the urban jungles of the developed world.

When autumn comes, Esmeralda puts a spell of slumber over her world, allowing it to rest until the spring. She will indulge in a long sleep through the cold season, curling up in a secret grotto. She glows like dragon's gold moss and is protected from harm by the Cave Fairy. In the spring Esmeralda awakes, reinvigorated, ready to celebrate nature's rebirth. The cryptic rings and patterns she traces in the meadows can be seen from afar and only the Sun, Star and Moon Fairies have the power to decipher them.

Esmeralda's spirit is as delicate as dandelion fluff swaying in the breeze, yet at the sight of Earth's most valuable resources dwindling at the hands of a few greedy humans, her serenity is shattered. The rich malachite hue of her skin will suddenly turn a vitriolic shade of yellow. She enlists the help of her fairy friends to avenge those who betray the natural order. From devasting floods to blazing fires, destructive hurricanes or even mighty earthquakes, Esmeralda sends explicit warnings to the human world of the dire consequences of wastefulness and pollution.

Earthling Magic

 Stand outside with your bare feet on the grass in a park, garden, field or forest. Take a couple of minutes to inhale deeply, focusing on your breath. Try to visualise a root growing from your feet deep into the ground and connecting within the Earth. As you feel this connection strengthen, draw in Esmeralda's serene energy and feel it filling your mind with calm. Carry this green serenity with you throughout the rest of your day.

GREEN RESILIENCE
Mosses are plants that can grow in many different environments, from snowy mountains to hot deserts. They play an essential role in balancing the natural landscape by absorbing excess precipitation and retaining warmth when it gets cold or cooling off when temperatures rise. These thread-like plants are packed with chloroplasts that absorb light in order to produce sugar for fuel.

HIGH-GLOSS MOSS
Some mosses appear to shine in the dark thanks to evolutionary adaptations that have allowed these plants to thrive in the darkness – even in caves. One of the most famous cave mosses is known as dragon's gold, whose green glow is attributed to lens-shaped cells reflecting light that has been accumulated by the chloroplasts. In Hokkaido, Japan, there is a spectacular cave that is widely known for its luminescent dragon's gold.

PLANT PEOPLE
The moss people of German and Scandinavian legend are small, fairy-like creatures, who dwell in the forest and wear moss as clothing. Malevolent at times, the Moosfräulein could call a plague upon a household, but they could also save someone from a grave illness with an assortment of medicinal herbs. Related to mythical tree spirits, their goal is to protect the natural realm from humans.

EARTH FAIRIES

THE CAVE FAIRY

NIAH

This solitary creature retreated long ago to the enigmatic confines of her stony kingdom. She has raised the many hills and mountains of our planet and filled them with towering stalactites and glimmering chandeliers of salt. Using the mysterious fae alphabet of runes, Niah has inscribed millions of years of galactic history onto cave walls across the Universe.

Niah is the world's first painter and sculptor, translating her artistic vision to the rocky interiors of the Earth. She has inspired human artists to create their own compositions on stone, marble, paper and canvas, keeping the world's ancient arts alive. Her own paintings conjure up a menagerie of giant bears, dragons and griffins, weaving earthly truths together with fantasy.

Of all the fae, Niah is the richest. Her coffers are filled with gold, silver, copper and iron drawn from deep within the Earth, where her endless network of caves can disorientate even the most experienced of explorers. But Niah is a generous fairy and will share her fortune with any traveller intrepid or brave enough to scale the heady heights of her mountain lair.

Inside her cavernous abode, a swirling rainbow of diamonds, rubies, emeralds and sapphires dances across the walls in the candlelight. Delicately, Niah plucks these jewels from her walls, polishing and setting them until they sparkle on her neck, fingers and wrists, and dazzle in her magnificent crown.

Niah has taught the secrets of astronomy to countless human generations, revealing the metaphysical mysteries of the Earth and the sky. As the chief architect of the fae, she has led the construction of humankind's monumental stone tributes to nature – all the way from Stonehenge to Rapa Nui (also known as Easter Island).

Though she rarely ventures beyond her home, the Cave Fairy has been known to join the fae festivities on the solstice, peering out of watery coves to watch the Fairies of the Oceans and Seas dance on the moonlit waves of the Atlantic.

Rock of Favours

Find and clean a small rock, then decorate it with gold or yellow paint. When the paint is dry, draw the Cave Fairy's symbol on it. Now clasp it in the palm of your hand and, ideally on a night when the Moon is waxing and in a place where there is an echo, chant the following:

Niah, fairy of the most wonderous caves, bring me luck to obtain what my heart truly craves.

MONUMENTAL TIMES

Standing stone structures such as megaliths, menhirs, stelae, tumuli and dolmens are monumental sites deliberately set into the ground by early humans. These massive stones are typically set in a line, a group of lines or a circle, oval or semicircle formation. They are believed to have served as a meeting place, a ceremonial location for communal rituals as well as lookout points for defence – and even as a sort of celestial clock and calendar. At around 12,000 years old, the most ancient standing stone structure is believed to be Gobekli Tepe in modern-day Turkey.

PREHISTORIC PAINTERS

The oldest known cave paintings date back 43,000–65,000 years, and include the caves of La Pasiega, Maltravieso and Ardales in Spain, and the Maros-Pangkep caves of Indonesia. Using red or black pigment made from iron oxides, manganese dioxide and charcoal, these prehistoric artists used their fingers or simple tools to create both abstract designs and figurative images of animals, including pigs, bisons, rabbits, lions, deer, rhinos, giraffes, mammoths, and even humans. Other famous prehistoric cave paintings have been found around the world, offering a glimpse of how our planet's landscape has changed.

MOUNTAIN QUEEN

Ana, the Fairy Queen of Romany lore, lived in a mountain castle with her cohort of magical spirits called Keshalyi. Her peaceful existence was shattered when an evil Earth-dwelling spirit set out to destroy her beloved Keshalyi when she refused his advances. To save them from a tragic fate, she agreed to marry him and suffered years of misery by his side. She eventually escaped his monstrous grip and returned to her castle in shame, living in solitude and taking on the form of a golden toad on the rare occasions she ventured out of her cavernous refuge.

EARTH FAIRIES

THE MOUSE FAIRY

SORELLA

A permanent spell of mousehood has rendered this fairy unquestionably adorable, with a velvety pair of ears at the top of her head and a snow-white set of protruding front teeth.

Dressed in a sumptuous coat of sleek fur, Sorella travels the globe collecting the fallen milk teeth of children. Indeed, her alternate guise as the Tooth Fairy keeps her busy after sunset. She quietly creeps into the homes of children who have placed their teeth under their pillow in the hope that she will come and exchange their pearly whites for a lovely trinket or some gold coins.

She rides a flying bicycle, zooming through the skies to deliver gifts piled high in her basket. Given her nocturnal lifestyle, she has an excellent sense of smell, which helps her make her way to each destination, despite her poor eyesight. As soon as she receives the signal that an earthly child has lost a tooth, she slips in and swiftly makes the switch. Every tooth she acquires is precious and the Mouse Fairy tucks her treasures into a leather pouch that hangs off her belt.

Despite her high-powered career, Sorella is still quite a timid creature. She will scamper off instantly at the first sight of a human. However, if a child leaves her a glass of milk or a biscuit, she may linger a moment or two. At the end of each night, just before sunrise, Sorella stashes all the teeth she has collected in a forest burrow. She then casts a spell to ask for each child's future to be firmly rooted in the Earth, as they embark on the next phase of their journey from infancy to adolescence.

As dawn approaches, she sweeps through the towns and the enchanted fields of the countryside as noiselessly as she can. She checks up on all her forest friends in their slumber, before curling up in her mousey underground home to catch up on some much-needed rest before the Moon rises anew.

Dreamy Daisies

If you have a toothache, pick up three daisies and pop them underneath your pillow. The Mouse Fairy will find them and cast a soothing spell for you to sleep well. Wearing a daisy chain crown during the day can also help ease the discomfort of a toothache.

SHARP SENSES
While many nocturnal animals have quite good eyesight, mice can't see very well in the dark. Instead, they rely on the excellent hearing their big ears afford them and an impeccable sense of smell. Combined with the sensory information they get from the whiskers on their snouts, mice are adept at getting around at night.

ENDLESS TEETHING
Like other rodents, mice have teeth that keep growing. They wear down and renew their four front teeth roughly every forty days by nibbling, chewing and grinding them down. That is why mice like to chew on various objects when they visit houses – as opposed to cheese which, contrary to popular opinion, they aren't actually too fond of.

MOUSEY ROOTS
One of the most legendary tales of the Mouse Fairy was written by Madame d'Aulnoy in the seventeenth century. A benevolent fairy known as La Petite Souris transforms into a mouse to defeat an evil king and shield his innocent daughter. The fairy protects the princess as she grows up and saves her from a catastrophic fate.

EARTH FAIRIES

THE MOON FAIRY

LUNELLA

In the evening, Lunella rises from her fairy castle on the Moon to illuminate the night sky. She is the force that keeps our world in balance, staying in perfect rhythm with the Earth across the cosmic ballroom of the galaxy.

Lunella is independent and unpredictable, showing her many faces and moods throughout all 28 days of the lunar cycle. She tends to get grumpy when she hasn't had enough rest, especially on the morning after a full moon. Yet, she has a right to be exhausted after dancing the night away with her cousins, Marina and the Sea Fairies, and swimming along the tides that ebb and flow on her command.

Lunella is the fairy of self-reflection, healing and renewal. She sings gentle songs of happy dreams to children in their sleep, helping the Dream Fairy chase away nightmares with her moonstone wand. When the dawn comes, she greets the Sun Fairy, who arrives to take her place in the sky.

Twice a year, on the equinox, Lunella and the Sun Fairy stay up together to sing, dance and play all day and night. They concoct a special elixir exclusively for this celebration: a nectar made of freshly squeezed moon and sun rays. Just before dawn, they share their favourite stories of day and night, revealing the slumbering secrets of the world. On rare occasions, they get so excited that they bump into each other! This causes a total eclipse when day and night become one for an instant.

If you are lucky, you might encounter Lunella on a Blue Moon. Keep an eye out past midnight and you may spot her silver hair flashing across the sky. As her moondust wings flutter, she might be sipping moondew from an angel's trumpet or skipping upon your windowsill in search of moonflowers and moonstones to add to her collection.

Wish Upon the Moon

If you would like to share a special wish with the Moon Fairy, wait for the next new moon phase. Write it down on a piece of paper and place it on the windowsill or somewhere safe outside for Lunella to find. Once she discovers it, she will do everything in her power to make your wish come true by the time the moon cycle is complete.

MOON DAY
Humans have been worshipping the Sun, Moon, stars and planets for millennia. The days of the week in the Gregorian calendar come from the names of Norse and Roman gods and the celestial bodies they represent. In English, the word for Monday comes from the ancient Anglo-Saxon word 'mondandaeg', which also translates to 'the moon's day'.

LUNAR MANORS
There are unusual structures on the Moon that astronomers have dubbed 'fairy castles'. Researchers believe these strange peaks formed from the ice found in the cold, dark regions near the Moon's poles. While most of the water that reaches the lunar surface is quickly dissipated, ice at the poles takes the form of a fairy castle since these regions are perpetually freezing cold.

GLOWING GODDESS
In Chinese tradition, there were once ten suns in the sky, but no Moon and no night. One day, a skilled archer named Hou Yi used his bow to shoot down one of the suns. He was given an elixir of immortality as a reward. When his wife Chang'e discovered his secret, she drank the elixir and ascended into the sky. She became the eternal Moon Goddess, with only a pet rabbit for company.

EARTH FAIRIES

LUNELLA'S GUIDE...

The powerful relationship between our planet and its Moon influences much of life on Earth. Fairies work with the Moon's natural magic to achieve goals, manifest intentions and make wishes come true, with guidance from the Moon Fairy. Here are some of Lunella's tips on how to use the luminous properties of the Moon to bring more magic into your own life.

Waning Crescent

Rest: This is a time to recharge. Let your mind be still and go with the flow.

Last Quarter

Release: Let go of any habits and beliefs that might be holding you back. Note down your thoughts in a journal to see how far you've come.

Waning Gibbous

Contemplation: Reflect and look inwards to re-evaluate your intentions and goals for the next cycle.

Full Moon

Gratitude: While the Moon's energy is at its most powerful, thank nature for the gifts and learnings in your life.

ONCE IN A BLUE MOON

The 13th full moon happens on rare occasions, approximately once every three years. Named the Blue Moon, it marks an especially magical period in Faedom and on Earth, when many things that seem impossible can become a reality.

WISH UPON A BLOOD MOON

A total lunar eclipse is sometimes called a Blood Moon because of the appearance of a reddish tint on the full moon when it passes into the Earth's shadow.

New Moon
Intentions: Think of fresh ideas and set goals for what you would like to achieve this month.

Waxing Crescent
Action: Now is the time to start new projects that will allow you to achieve the goals you've set.

First Quarter
Perseverance: Keep going and don't be afraid to tackle any challenges that appear along the way.

Waxing Gibbous
Growth: Consider the positive results from the intentions you set out at the start and keep building on these accomplishments.

The Earth and the Moon are tidally locked, which means we can only ever see one side of the Moon as it orbits its host planet. The Moon's phases are determined by the angle of sunlight reflected on its surface as it circles around us throughout the lunar month.

...TO THE MOON

WATER FAIRIES

MARINA: THE SEA FAIRY
NEPHELIE: THE MIST & STEAM FAIRY
ONDINE: THE RIVERS & LAKES FAIRY
ISA: THE SNOW & ICE FAIRY
TALIA: THE RAIN & DEW FAIRY
SKYLAR: THE RAINBOW FAIRY

Water Fairies

The magic of the Water Fairies is a fresh, cleansing force that awakens the senses and imbues the Earth with life and wonder. Their gift of precious hydration allows us earthly creatures to thrive, ensuring the survival of every species of flora and fauna on our planet. These fairies are fluid, intuitive and empathetic, often absorbing the emotions flowing around them. Their moods can range from a languid trickle of serenity to a rushing stream of enthusiasm or even a thundering wave of anger. They are prone to bouts of melancholy, drowning their sorrows until they are ready to rise again. In the light of the Sun, they scintillate with all the colours of the rainbow reflected in their prismatic spirits. In icier climes, they grow more earnest and even solemn, their fluid spirits freezing into indomitable icicles. Wielding the rare power to create and destroy, the Water Fairies are especially pure of heart and their intentions tend to be as transparent as a glacial stream.

THE OCEANS & SEAS FAIRY
MARiNA

Rising from the furthest depths of the Atlantic Ocean, Marina is guardian of the Earth's oceans and seas. Her prodigious powers give her absolute control over all the creatures who inhabit her aquatic kingom.

Marina and her Sea Fairies prefer to linger below the surface of their watery lair. When they do emerge, the Sun glistens on their skin and lights up their decadent crowns of burnished coral and iridescent pearl. Some explorers have mistaken the Sea Fairies for mermaids, but they have legs instead of the fish tails sported by their ancient cousins.

Marina is proud and her temper can be cataclysmic. Overprotective of her kingdom, she demands absolute loyalty from all her water-dwelling subjects. She won't hesitate to send them out on hazardous missions to pluck rare shipwreck treasures from the sea floor. If she is feeling generous, Marina may leave a few of these enchanted artefacts in tidal pools for a lucky seafarer to discover.

As capricious as the waves, the Sea Fairies tend to argue amongst themselves, and when their quarrelling escalates, Marina steps in, crushing their arguments with devastating waves. Searching for precious loot, mythical sea creatures will lurk in the aftermath of these catastrophes, and an exasperated Marina will create terrifying whirlpools to scare these tricksters away.

Every evening, accompanied by her cortège of fairies, Marina consults with the Moon Fairy to ensure the smooth running of the tides. Astride her water horse, Aughisky, whose hooves beat a line of foam across the waves, she inspects her dominion. At any sign of threat to the ocean's bounty, she quickly summons her cohorts. Their enchanting voices, soothing like a gentle wave or unbearably shrill like a crashing wind, beguile those who dare intrude upon the ocean's precious ecosystem.

Smashing Sandcastles

If you are worried or frightened about something, build a sandcastle as the tide is rising. You can build as many as you want. As you build each sandcastle, think of what is worrying you. As the sea topples the castle over, repeat the words:

Sea, beautiful sea, banish my worries and let my mind be free.

SUNKEN RELICS
There are more than three million sunken ships spread across the ocean floor, many of them containing ancient objects and treasures. Among the most famous hoards reported to date is the Uluburun shipwreck, discovered off the coast of Turkey and thought to be over 3,000 years old. It took nearly a decade to gather up the cache of gold, silver, jewels and weapons stashed on board.

TIDAL TANGO
Tides are caused by the gravitational pull of the Moon on our planet, causing a pair of bulges that originate where the Earth is widest and thus closest to the Moon. As the Earth spins, different areas of the oceans face the Moon and flow into the bulge, causing water levels to rise when an area is inside a bulge and fall when it moves out. These tidal cycles drive ocean currents, regulating global temperatures and climate.

SEA SPIRIT
As the patron of the fishermen of Brazil, Yemanjá (also known as 'Janaina') originates from Nigeria, where the Yoruba people believe in spiritual elemental beings known as Orishas. During the New Year celebrations in Rio de Janeiro, thousands of people gather on the beach in Copacabana to make offerings of candles and flowers. In exchange, she offers them luck and prosperity.

WATER FAIRIES

THE MIST & STEAM FAIRY

NEPHELIE

A most intrepid and industrious fairy, Nephelie combines elements of nature and technology to invent new instruments and contraptions. Born with just one leg, she has used her engineering prowess to create a mechanical limb, which allows her to move faster than any other being in the fairy realm.

Nephelie's house is built of riveted metal, with an enormous domed roof. Hot steamy springs flow inside her residence, filling fountains and waterfalls that feed exotic green plants and orchids. An enormous aviary harbours all sorts of injured birds and formidable creatures, which Nephelie takes great care to repair with new wings and beaks. Once recovered, they are either released back into the wild or given sanctuary in her home.

Fierce when she needs to be, Nephelie's temper will rise to a boil and explode in a burst of noxious fumes. She confuses and distracts offenders with a puff of dark smog so thick that travellers may find themselves completely disoriented. Indeed, legend has it that she is responsible for hiding the mysterious Isle of Avalon from human sight behind a thick wall of mist. When this formidable fairy is sad, her tears fall as a misty drizzle upon the world.

When in playful and creative mode, the Mist and Steam Fairy will fill the sky with fluffy cumulus clouds in all sorts of amusing shapes or play light-hearted pranks on the Wind and Storm Fairies. She travels to the human realm by hot-air balloon, which she navigates with great agility, her hair flowing in the wind. She often visits flea markets to find treasures, trinkets and spare parts for her next engineering project. Her cloudy eyes sharpen to a dark brown when she spots a particularly useful item.

Though some feel she defies the laws of nature, Nephelie's engineering feats sustain and mend the marvels of the natural world with the sole intention to create a better and more wondrous abode for both human and fae. Her nebulous form might make her hard to spot, but you may catch her in the steam that rises from a boiling kettle, and she is known to leave behind messages, symbols and love letters on foggy mirrors and windows for anyone looking for inspiration.

Misty Mirror Message

If you are nervous about something, after a warm shower, use your finger to write a couple of words to describe the object of your fear on the steamed-up bathroom mirror. Then trace the Mist and Steam Fairy's symbol next to your message. As it vanishes, you will feel Nephelie's energy ease your anxiety.

WATER POWER

Steam has been used to power mechanical devices since antiquity, but in the seventeenth century the first commercial steam-powered pump was invented. While steam is non-toxic, fuels used to heat the water can lead to the release of toxic gases. Scientists believe that switching to organic waste materials could provide a climate-friendly alternative.

KASUMI

In Japanese art, there is a tradition of depicting horizontal or vertical mists in paintings, known as Kasumi. They denote a transition in time or a passing into a world of fantasy. One of the most well-known painters to have worked in this style is Katsushika Hokusai. Bound by travel restrictions in Tokyo (then known as Edo), Hokusai never left the city. He imagined fantastical realms, which are portrayed in his works.

MISTY MYSTERY

The mystical Isle of Avalon is veiled by heavy fog, and is said to be guarded by the Lady of the Lake and her fairies. This magical enclave is home to the most beautiful fruits, flowers and vegetation. Any mortal privileged enough to visit would be spellbound by its magnificence. It is believed that the legendary King Arthur lies there, waiting until he returns to rule again.

WATER FAIRIES

THE RIVERS & LAKES FAIRY

ONDINE

A flood of happy tears from the Rain and Dew Fairy whipped up by the blizzard of the Snow and Ice Fairy has given life to Ondine. Gathering each precious drop trickling down the mountain, she forms pools and ponds, rivers and streams that meander through forests, fields and cities.

Hopping between her ponds and lakes, Ondine greets fishes and frogs as she peers into the murkiest of swamps and bogs to make sure that everything is in order. She flies along the edge of the water, scattering bouquets of her water lilies, mixed in with reeds that sway in the breeze, creating a glorious aquatic kingdom for all the creatures of the water. On summer evenings, she travels to nearby towns to collect coins from the depths of magical fountains and wells, granting wishes for those who tossed them in with earnest intentions. She sews each coin under her skirt, which swishes musically every time she moves.

Ondine guards her realm by drawing on the power of water, casting curses on the witches and sprites who lurk at the bottom of certain haunted lakes, intent on luring humans into their traps. Ondine also offers protection to the wildlife around her, restoring balance in the water cycle when something has gone awry. She and her army of badgers and beavers clear the banksides of rubbish and pollution, punishing those who litter by making the mud in certain places just a bit more slippery than usual.

To replenish the seas and oceans, Ondine carries water all the way to the land's edge, where she may dawdle to regale Marina and the Seas Fairies with epic stories from her watery abode. Ondine has a flair for the tragic and will often find herself entangled in the complicated affairs of humans. She has helped many heroes on their quests, even gifting the sword Excalibur to the legendary Pendragon kings. She holds the secrets to the location of the Holy Grail, though she will only share her knowledge with the most noble of knights.

Though her heart has borne the heavy wounds of unrequited love from her adventures, Ondine finds solace in the calming flow of running water. She gifts the Earth with her cleansing magic and gives any human who bathes in her rivers and lakes the possibility of adventure and triumph.

Lustrous Looking-glass

For problem solving, or to get a glimpse into the future, use this spell during the new moon. Fill a non-metallic bowl with water, sit in a quiet place in the evening, whisper your request to Ondine while gazing into the water and breathing deeply. Then write down any thoughts no matter how strange. With practice, you will access Ondine's wisdom and intuition.

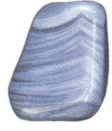

Fairy with the clearest mind and purest heart, reveal the knowledge that only you can impart!

WATER MEMORY

Homeopaths and scientists alike have long claimed that water has a memory of its own. Water can retain a 'recollection' of a substance, even after the original molecules have disappeared through dilution. This theory has been the basis for many remedies, whereby certain natural substances are diluted in order to enhance their therapeutic properties.

SACRED SPRINGS

Pilgrims have been flocking to spa sanctuaries for centuries to seek peace and healing. In France, the Grotto of Massabielle attracts about six million people every year, who come to pay their respects to Our Lady of Lourdes. The custom began in 1858, when the young Bernadette Soubirous had a miraculous vision. Since then, these waters have been famed for their sacred and healing properties.

NAUGHTY NYMPHS

The Nixies of Germanic folklore are beguiling water nymphs residing in ponds and lakes. During the summer solstice, they venture out to join balls and parties and entice young men to dance. Transfixed, these men often follow them to their aquatic dominion, only to perish in deadly waters. A nymph can be spotted by the wet hem of her ballgown.

WATER FAIRIES

THE SNOW & ICE FAIRY
ISA

This fairy adores the winter season – skating over frozen ponds, climbing the highest peaks and skiing down never-ending slopes, gliding from pole to pole across the most glacial of Earth's expanses. Her mere touch has the power to freeze just about anything, creating lustrous icicles and sculptures that shimmer in the light of the Moon.

Isa always travels with her pets – a snowy owl and a cunning, colour-changing fox. The pair had once been human, before they fell victim to a curse cast on them by a malevolent winter spirit. Many times, Isa has tried to undo the curse and set her loyal friends free, but to no avail. When Isa sleeps, her owl circles her, stretching his magnificent wings as he watches over her and her dominion. Meanwhile, the fox scours the snow-capped pine forests in pursuit of any scheming enemies.

As guardian of the poles and their endangered fauna, Isa fiercely defends her icy home, stretching a blanket of frost across the hemisphere as soon as autumn has ended. Her fury at the sight of the ancient ice of the Arctic and Antarctic disappearing causes snowstorms to flash across the sky and whip across the Earth. To protect her realm, Isa has been known to run ships aground, and her infamous frosty bite results in a painful death for those who thwart her.

As Yuletide and the New Year approach, Isa's playful side comes alive. During this time, she ventures closer to the human world, warming her frosty palms on the festive beacons and fires that light up the darkness, her cheeks turning pink as she gallivants across fields of snow, leaving behind an outline of her wondrous fairy form.

When spring arrives, Isa retreats to her towering castle of ice and mirrors. These halls of infinite reflections have allowed her to peer into the realms of both human and fae to glimpse their destinies and intentions, catching whispers of wishes that she will grant to those deserving her assistance. Given her knack for stopping dead in her tracks at the sight of people, Isa is often mistaken for an ice sculpture by human folk.

Ice Breaker

If you find yourself wanting to make a new friend but are feeling rather shy, try this spell. Pour strawberry or elderflower juice in an ice tray and set it in the freezer. Invite a new friend over and add one of your colourful ice cubes to your cups. Before you take a sip, chant the words:

Isa, lend us your crystalline magic to break the ice and forge new friendships.

EMPRESS OF ICE

Russian sovereign Anna Ivanovna had a sumptuous palace built in St Petersburg. It was fully fitted with furnishings made entirely of ice. This construction was a technical marvel for the eighteenth century, though its history reveals some rather cruel intentions. The empress was against the love match between a Russian prince and an Italian lady, so she made the couple spend their wedding night in the bitter cold of this magnificent yet precarious edifice. Her hope was that they would both freeze to death. Fortunately, Anna's elaborate ploy didn't work, and they both survived. The palace has since melted away.

PLANETARY COOLING

The snow and ice that covers the north and south poles helps balance the Earth's temperature by reflecting some of the Sun's heat back into space. When these ice caps start melting, it can cause extreme disruptions in weather patterns and lead to heatwaves in the summer and freezing temperatures in winter, as well as severe flooding and ferocious storms. This is why climate activists are fighting against fossil fuels and greenhouse emissions which heat up the planet, to put a halt to these destructive effects. Little steps can help, such as making sure to switch off the lights when leaving a room, or having showers instead of baths.

MOUNTAIN MUSE

There are numerous variations on the Japanese myth of Yuki-Onna, a spirit known to take on the form of a beautiful ageless woman. She lives in the cold mountains and is associated with snow and ice. Yuki-Onna is sometimes portrayed as benevolent, offering joy to the less fortunate, however these pleasures would be as fleeting as a snowflake in one's palm. Other tales depict her as a fierce and vengeful creature with the power to make travellers get stuck in the snow, preventing them from returning home. Cold water will make her bulge and swell, while hot water can make her disappear altogether.

WATER FAIRIES

THE
RAIN & DEW FAIRY

Talia

Sensitive by nature, Talia is ruled by her emotions and wears her heart on her sleeve. At the very hint of sorrow, her eyes will fill with tears. Her pupils glitter, bright as silver, and crystal-clear droplets spill from behind her lashes and fall in gentle rivulets to the fields and forests of Earth. Talia's rich emotion nourishes plants and wildlife, fills wells and replenishes rivers.

Each day, Talia bursts out of her slumbering bubble, ready to offer the bees, butterflies, beetles, ants and spiders their sustenance, quenching their morning thirst with her sparkling beads of moisture. For the flowers, she traces each petal with a touch of pure water. And so, Talia ensures that all Earth's creatures have plenty to drink.

Talia may cause drizzle when in a grump and bicker with the Mist and Steam Fairy, creating foggy mornings. When she feels mysterious, she will trace a vague haze through the skies. When Talia is feeling furious, she can provoke torrential rains and sow panic. Even when she is merry, Talia often laughs until she cries, causing sporadic showers. In mischievous mode, she might rain on the day of a parade and even conjure a downpour in the middle of a garden wedding. In her defence, Talia does consider rain a good omen for the future.

Easily offended, especially when she is insulted by the brazen outbursts of the Fire Fairies, Talia waddles about in a puddle of gloom, until she has gathered her thoughts. Only the Rainbow Fairy has the power to cheer Talia up, taking her on colourful escapades through Faedom to shake off her melancholy. Sometimes, Talia will hide from the world for weeks until she is summoned back by the pleas of a parched Earth. Together with a team of weather spirits known as Kokos, she replenishes the rains and dewdrops that keep our planet alive.

Despite her many moods, Talia always loves her work hydrating and cooling down the flora and fauna of the Earth. On the first of May, she may even bestow the gift of dewy and youthful skin to any human who washes their face in the dew of hawthorn leaves. Her physical form is not easy to spot, but a splash of her spirit is contained in every drop of rain and dew.

Rain Dance

If it hasn't rained in days and you feel that the natural world around you needs a dose of Talia's hydrating magic, you can perform your own rain dance. On your own or with friends, you can find a song you like or even make one up. Form a circle and dance your heart out, chanting the following phrase:

*Talia, spirit of rain and dew,
let your healing force be renewed.*

SCENT SENSE

Through the hydrologic cycle, the salty water of the seas and oceans evaporates and rises into the sky, leaving the salt behind. Warmed by sunlight, these water droplets form clouds, and eventually come back down as rain. When it rains, we often sense a distinctive smell in the air. Called 'petrichor', it is the result of organic material breaking down and fusing with soil, rocks and minerals.

DEWY DRINK

Dewdrops are a nifty way to keep plants hydrated, especially in hot environments. As the air cools down overnight, vapour condenses into droplets that settle onto the surfaces of plants. This dew forms a protective barrier, locking moisture in and keeping the plant hydrated. Over the course of the day, as the air warms up, the remaining dew evaporates, helping to keep the plant cool.

MORNING ELIXIR

During the reign of the Han dynasty in China, morning dew was collected in jade cups for members of the court. Jade was believed to prolong life and the stone's virtue would increase the dew's potency, making it a valuable elixir. In Europe, the Ellefolk of Danish folklore used to lick dew from plants in the morning as it was the only substance that they believed could safely nourish and hydrate them.

WATER FAIRIES

THE RAINBOW FAIRY

SKYLAR

Swift-footed Skylar whizzes across the sky in a burst of sparkling colour, leaping through the air in a wave of joy and radiance. One of the fastest fairies, they glide from city to city on their magical roller skates, with their unicorn Iris galloping swiftly behind.

Never one to miss a good party, Skylar can be spotted at all kinds of festivities. Emerging from a cloud of multi-coloured confetti, streamers and ribbons, they will disappear into the singing, dancing throng. They're always an honoured guest at birthday parties, especially when their favourite rainbow cake is being served.

Gleeful and daring, Skylar enjoys showing off their acrobatic abilities, and their circus of stunts always leaves their audiences in awe. Their death-defying tricks bend light at a whim, flipping and twisting rainbow batons and tucking them into clusters of clouds. Their unicorn may offer a fellow fairy a ride on its back as they rush through the sky like a living rollercoaster. The fairies hold on tight, shrieking and giggling in delight.

Skylar's personality is as nuanced and layered as the rainbow itself – rippling like water, blazing like fire and flowing like the wind. Always looking for excuses to dip down to Earth – if only for a minute – they navigate their many moods with ease, never dwelling on any mishap for too long, and embracing their individuality. Skylar encourages all fae to embrace the unique parts of themselves that make them stand out.

Together with the Bird Fairy, Skylar's more serious role is to relay messages between the spirit and earthly realms, building bridges between the two worlds and creating a multi-coloured pathway for travelling between the two. They also deliver important news from the human world to the fae who are loathe to leave their realm.

Since time began, mortals have been searching for the end of the rainbow, hoping to find treasure, or their heart's desire, at its source. Skylar's mission is to ensure that no ill-intentioned being may cross the magical boundary that separates the Earth from Faedom.

Rainbow Mandala

Relax your mind and set your creativity free by making your own mandala. Take a piece of paper and draw a small circle as a base, then start adding geometric shapes around the circle. Build on each layer with different shapes, using the colours that represent your mood: red for power, orange for creativity, yellow for energy, green for health, blue for calm, indigo for wisdom and violet for motivation.

COLOUR WHEEL

When we spot a rainbow in the sky, we see just a portion of the colourful halo that appears when sunlight passes through water droplets and gets broken up into its individual hues. If you were to fly up above the rainbow in an aeroplane, you would be able to see it as a complete circle made up of concentric rings in all the colours in the spectrum.

RAY OF HOPE

For centuries, the rainbow has been used as a symbol of hope and happiness. During the German Peasants' War in the sixteenth century, the rainbow served as a symbol for the cooperative movement. Since the 1970s, it has represented the movement for LGBTQ+ rights across the world. Its many colours manifest the diversity of its community and the broad spectrum of human love and gender.

MAGIC MESSAGES

The Greek messenger goddess, Iris, was also the personification of the rainbow. When gods were to take a solemn oath, she would fill a large jug with water from the River Styx. If they lied, the water would put them to sleep for a year. In the *Iliad*, Homer describes how Iris carried messages and advice between the gods and humans during the Trojan War.

ANATOMY OF

Lunula
Crescent-shaped wing marking

LIVING COLOURS

Fairy wings are covered in microscopic scales that reflect a full spectrum of colour, from the optical to the ultraviolet. Their structure resembles that of a photonic crystal, which means that they refract white light to reveal other bright colours, as well as a spectacular iridescence that makes the wings glow. Their ultraviolet patterns can be seen by other fairies and certain animals, but are invisible to humans.

Ocellus
Eye-shaped wing marking

FAIRY WINGS

Forewing
Larger and more powerful top wing, used to propel flight

FEATHERS AND FLAMES
Fairy wings usually resemble those of a butterfly or moth, but other types of fairy wings may be soft like flower petals, feathered like a bird's plumage, scaly like reptile skin, flowing like water or flickering like flames. These wings can also be utterly transparent or full of colour.

Hindwing
These lower wings are less powerful but can help to take tight turns in the air

FIRE FAIRIES

SOLANGE: THE SUN FAIRY

SERAPHINA: THE LAVA FAIRY

FARAH: THE DESERT FAIRY

ALMA: THE KITCHEN FAIRY

AKARI: THE NEON FAIRY

ASTER: THE STAR FAIRY

Fire Fairies

Igniting the earthly realm with their blazing magic, the Fire Fairies wield a tremendous and explosive power. Their passionate flames have guided humankind through the dark since the beginning of time, endowing us with the gift of fire, warming the hearth and illuminating the path to joy, wisdom and discovery. Radiant and playful, they journey through the skies in a festive cavalcade of lights. It's not all fun and games in the realm of fire, since the fairies' tempers often flare. Their fury bursts forth like lava, scorching everything for miles around. They cannot be assuaged until the Air and Water Fairies flow in to restore the natural balance among the elements. Flickering between joy and ire, these volatile spirits are the light of the world, born of the spark that appeared in the sky in the first few seconds of cosmic time.

THE SUN FAIRY

SOLANGE

Fairy queen of the sun-kissed skies, Solange is all-powerful and the centre of everything, holding up the balance of the world and giving vital life to all things.

Rising in the east, she appears as a soft glow at dawn, giving a nonchalant signal to the Moon Fairy to retire so that she may revel in her solitary glory. With every minute of the morning, she glows brighter. Slowly, she awakens each little corner of the world with her gentle kisses of heat and light, urging the Flower Fairies to perk up their petals and get to work, reminding the Kitchen Fairy that it's time to start warming up the hearth.

Though her glow is comforting, her touch is scorching – as those who live near the Earth's equator know all too well. Her blazing strength can parch the land and blight the harvest. And when Solange is angry, she may dry up lakes and rivers, ignite forests and melt the ice off the highest peaks. The pleas of the Wind and Storm Fairies can cool her temper, and the Water Fairies may shower their magic across the sky to stamp out her fires, or block her out with clouds. But it is only Lunella the Moon Fairy who can truly soothe Solange's fiery nature. Together, they dance through the Universe in a cosmic ballet, casting shadow and light on the Earth.

Solange's favourite day to shine is the summer solstice. In celebration she will stretch out the day as far as possible and take over the night. The whole world rejoices as she lowers the magical veil that separates the human and fae realms, so that everyone may indulge in this extraordinary moment of seemingly eternal sunshine together.

When her day is nearly done, Solange saunters off to the west, her luminous sceptre in hand, and steps into her gilded chariot, bidding the world good night. Yet even when she disappears in one place, the Sun Fairy is still tirelessly carrying on to the next, without respite.

Radiant Ray Catcher

To capture some of Solange's luminous magic, upcycle any kind of clear box, even the sort you buy fruit in. You will also need scissors, colourful permanent markers, a hole punch, string or ribbon, and a small twig. Cut out three circles of plastic and colour them with the markers; you can even draw Solange's symbol on them. Punch small holes in each circle and tie each piece to a twig with string or ribbons. Hang the twig off another string or thread and let Solange's luminous presence energise you.

ALMIGHTY STAR

The Sun is among the largest and hottest stars in our part of the Universe. The core temperature has been estimated at 15 million degrees Celsius. A huge amount of energy is produced by the Sun via fusion, emitted as heat, light and radiation. Our Sun has been shining for about 4.6 billion years and has enough fuel to keep shining for billions more.

BLACKOUT

Solar eclipses are unique events that occur when the Moon momentarily ends up between the Sun and Earth and blocks the light of the Sun from reaching us. During a total eclipse, the three bodies are in full alignment and the sky becomes dark. During a partial eclipse, the three are not aligned and the Sun appears to have a shadow covering part of its surface. Solar eclipses happen every 18 months or so.

ETERNAL SUN

The summer solstice has long been celebrated to mark the day when the Sun is believed to be at the peak of its power. Some believe that the veil between the fae and earthly realm is at its thinnest, facilitating travel between the two realms. Women would gather the blooms of St John's wort to ward off evil magic, and burn lavender to attract the favour of the fae.

THE LAVA FAIRY

SERAPHINA

From her volcanic lair, Seraphina erupts with a tremendous roar and a flash of fire, her scorching tresses leaving a trail of magma in her stead. Her eyes are a blazing topaz, with the power to petrify even the fiercest of humans.

Seraphina's volcanic eruptions allow the Earth to maintain a stable temperature and support life on our planet and nourish the soil. Her fiery nature offers the natural world the heat and spark that light up our lives. Yet the fury of her actions can often lead to massive explosions of magma and ash storms that carry enough might to bury an entire city.

Seraphina's temper can flare and she speaks her mind, no matter the consequences. She is guardian of the Earth's geothermal power and the protector of volcanoes across the globe. She travels the world – from Iceland to the Mediterranean hills, the tropical isles of Hawai'i and the Philippines all the way to Antarctica – skipping through the sulphuric peaks of the Rockies and the volcanic ridges of Africa. She dives deep under land and water to release the fire below, causing a hubbub of boiling bubbles that rise through the sea, feeding hot mineral springs and exploding into the air as geysers.

The kindness of the Lava Fairy may be just as intense as her anger. She endows the Earth with rich volcanic soil to bring abundant harvests. The extraordinary blooms of the bird of paradise and passionflower come from the cliffs of her thunderous mountains. In her volcanic lair, Seraphina builds forges and furnaces, crafting beautiful ironwork from the mineral riches that burst from the craters, as well as sparkling jewellery encrusted with precious stones. She generously shares her enchanted tools and treasures with her friends, chatting animatedly over a cup of sizzling hot mead.

Spotting Seraphina is nearly impossible without scaling the feverish heights of a volcanic mountain, but she is known to appear on Bonfire Night and at candlelight concerts. If you see a flash of blazing light in the sky, it could well be Seraphina.

Self-confidence Sigil

On a piece of paper, write down a few words using a positive statement in the present tense to set your intention. For example, 'I am confident'. Once you have done this, remove all the vowels. Arrange the remaining consonants however you like to create your own symbol. Intertwine the letters and embellish them with decorative accents. When you are happy with your symbol, ask Seraphina to infuse it with her fairy powers and let the magic flow.

FIRE & ASH
There are over 1,500 active volcanoes on our planet. Underwater volcanoes account for about 75 per cent of the active volcanoes on Earth. Every second, about 20 volcanoes erupt around the world. Though they can be devastating, these eruptions are vital to the geothermal processes that regulate the heat and pressure above and below the Earth's crust.

NOTORIOUS ERUPTION
Eyjafjallajökull is a famous Icelandic volcano that gained notoriety in 2010, when it ejected plumes so thick that aeroplanes couldn't fly near it. The intensity of the eruption has been attributed to the clash of hot magma inside the Earth against the cold water from glacial melt, suggesting that climate change may lead to more frequent volcanic eruptions in the future.

FLAMING ORIGINS
The word 'volcano' comes from the name of the Roman god of fire and forges, Vulcan. Volcanoes are typically associated with fiery emotions. One Aztec myth tells the story of two lovers who died tragically and were turned into volcanoes. Whenever the volcano Popacatepetl erupts, the warrior's passion for his beloved Iztaccihuatl is ignited.

FIRE FAIRIES

THE DESERT FAIRY

FARAH

The Desert Fairy appears across the golden haze of hot sand like a winged goddess, her pet cobra curled around her neck, hissing at the slightest sign of danger. Farah hushes his qualms with a lulling charm. As queen of the most treacherous realm on Earth, she fears no one.

A nomadic spirit, Farah leads a caravan of winged camels and dromedaries, griffins, sphinxes, many-headed lions and other trooping fairies across the Sahara and Death Valley, through the sandless Gobi Desert to the ochre-coloured outback of Australia. When the heat rises, they rest at an oasis formed by a fanciful whoosh of sand and dust. Here, in the lush shade of monumental palm trees, the Desert Fairy refreshes herself on dates and pomegranate juice, cooling her feet in crystal-clear waters. As night falls, the fairy cavalcade will fall asleep under a canopy of constellations.

Guardian of ancient artefacts, Farah ventures underground to visit cool desert caves carved with hieroglyphics, archaic spells and the tales she once whispered to the ancient storytellers. She hums incantations to protect age-old temples and pyramids, devising all sorts of traps to ward off greedy scavengers who might otherwise plunder her spoils. At night, Farah wanders museum corridors, trying on the ancient baubles of famous kings and queens. She retrieves stolen treasures and smuggles them out in the folds of her gowns to return them to their rightful owners.

She delights in the fervent company of her kind, especially the Lava Fairy, with whom she gossips and trades desert treasures for sparkling trinkets. But she does not take insults lightly. When her temper is tested, she will corral the Wind and Storm Fairies and whip up ferocious sandstorms against her enemies.

The Desert Fairy is known for creating the most incredible mirages, from towering palaces and golden cities, to cascading waterfalls and alluring treasures. These beguiling illusions can prove disorientating to the novice explorer. Succumbing to her power, many perish in the blistering heat of her realm.

Charmful Sparkle

When the Moon is waning, draw the Desert Fairy's symbol on a piece of paper and wrap it around a ring, bracelet, charm or anything else that is precious and shiny. Every time you wear it, you will get an extra boost of courage by chanting:

Farah, Desert Queen, please charge this trinket with your protection.

MIRAGE MAGIC

When light passes through layers of air at different temperatures, the effect is called a mirage. In the desert, the Sun heats the sand as well as the air above it, causing light rays to be refracted and appear 'bent'. From a distance, the colliding layers of air masses act as a mirror, often creating the impression of a body of water – an illusion that is, in fact, a reflected image of the sky. Countless exhausted and thirsty travellers have been tricked by mirages.

SUCCULENT OASES

In deserts, water is by far the most valuable resource. Oases are rare fertile areas that can either be human-made or appear naturally near a freshwater source. The Sahara Desert supports about ninety major oases, which vary in size, from a cluster of date palms surrounding a small spring to a whole city with irrigated fields. Some of the crops that grow in an oasis include cotton, dates, olives, figs, citrus fruits, wheat and corn.

DRAGON'S BREATH

The fairy rings of the Namib Desert are one of Africa's greatest mysteries, with thousands of sandy circles dotting the otherwise desolate landscape. The indigenous Himba people of Namibia believe these rings are formed by dancing fairies or other spirits. Some local legends even describe dragons lurking underneath the ground, whose noxious breath rises up to the surface in perfectly spherical puffs that have been imprinted onto the fiery sand.

THE KITCHEN FAIRY
ALMA

This fairy's spirit, ignited by the divine gift of fire, glows with the eternal warmth of a cook and a healer. With a spring in her step, she wanders her realm, enjoying chirpy conversation with all the creatures she meets.

Alma's secret kitchen, hidden deep in an enchanted clearing, is surrounded by a glorious garden filled with herbs, edible flowers, fruits and vegetables. Her dark, amber-flecked eyes sparkle as she concocts her potent recipes. Vibrant bubbles and steam rise from her pots and change colour, depending on the intensity of her magic.

Alma's cosy hearth is stocked with pots and jars labelled with the most peculiar names. She furiously dips, dashes and sprinkles a pinch of this and a handful of that into her recipes. She pickles, conserves, smokes and broils, and her brews bubble away happily in a giant cauldron. Anything she discards is composted and returned to her garden or gifted to a fortunate farmer.

She will gladly invite all sorts of wonderful beasts and beings to warm themselves by her fireplace, sharing stories and tales of her intrepid adventures. Fairies travel from far away to sample her healing potions and restorative ambrosias, all while indulging in sticky buns dipped in fountains of milk infused with her famous honey mead.

Warm and empathetic, Alma is always ready to comfort a friend or upset child. She eagerly rewards a worthy mortal with a healing poultice or a brew of fortune, but if someone dares to take advantage of her generosity, she will ensure the failure of any recipe. A stew will be too salty, a sauce will be too bitter and a cake will burn in the oven. Her tricks are never malicious, but they can leave an unpleasant taste that lingers for days. Fortunately for her foes, Alma does not hold a grudge for long and when the scales are balanced, she will happily move on.

Mystic Pizza

Herbs have different magical properties, and a fun way to benefit from their power is to sprinkle different types of herbs on a pizza. Call on Alma to infuse your ingredients with her magic. If you are looking for love and friendship, add dried basil, for luck and protection sprinkle oregano, while rosemary will improve your memory – a good one before an exam! If you want to ward off nasty bullies, parsley will do the trick, and if you seek courage, add a dash of thyme. Invite your friends for a pizza party and enjoy Alma's good favour.

CULINARY MAGIC

The process of cooking has the power to combine a mix of raw ingredients into a hearty meal. The chemistry of cooking – mixing, blending and heating – transforms basic ingredients, like flour, eggs, sugar and butter, into lovely cakes. Cooking certain vegetables also boosts their nutritional content so we end up absorbing more vital vitamins and minerals with each bite. Making magic in the kitchen and sharing meals with loved ones is one of the most valuable ways to take care of yourself and others.

HAPPY ACCIDENTS

In ancient Mesopotamia, a baker once left his dough in the rain and found that it had become a juicy fermented liquid, which we know today as beer. Throughout history, there have been countless culinary surprises. In the 1930s an American innkeeper called Ruth Wakefield didn't have enough chocolate for her biscuit dough, so she added broken bits from a chocolate bar to her dough believing it would melt, but instead she created the delicious chocolate chip cookie. It's more than likely the Kitchen Fairy has had something to do with many of these fortunate mistakes.

FAIRY GODMOTHER

In French folklore, legend has it that if the Kitchen Fairy finds an offering of bread or other treats underneath an oak tree, she will search for the closest house where a mother has given birth. She will bless the child with countless talents and gift the new mother with health and vigour, ensuring her pantry is always stocked with plenty of food. She will become the child's fairy godmother for life and protect it from other fairies who might attempt to steal it and replace it with a baby-like creature called a 'changeling'.

FIRE FAIRIES

THE NEON FAIRY

AKARI

Born of the aurora borealis, the Neon Fairy's electrifying spirit sweeps through the night with her super-charged guitar, spreading music and fireworks across the globe. Her skin gleams with a constellation of star tattoos and her flaming fluorescent hair crackles with a vivacious energy.

Accompanied by Raju, the legendary dog of lightning, Akari surfs the skies in pursuit of entertainment, picking up glow rocks along the way. Often spotted on the night life circuits of New York City, Paris and Tokyo, she also hosts Hong Kong's Symphony of Lights, sipping bright red bubble tea while lighting up a stream of neon signs. To cool off, she dives into the sea to play her magical guitar for her aquatic friends, her phosphorescence brightening even the murkiest waters.

In the darkest of hours of night, Akari's vibrant glow comforts those who may feel afraid. Her sparkling personality lends courage and energy to forlorn mortals and fae creatures alike. Akari's fluorescent beacons warn the fae and other magical creatures when danger is lurking, and she distracts the meddlesome Hinkypunks and Will o' the Wisps by luring them into bioluminescent traps. She is even audacious enough to frazzle the beguiling magic of monsters and tricksters to help her friends escape their grasp.

On fae holidays, Akari marches at the head of the fairy rade, jamming on her guitar. As the procession weaves through the woods and urban jungles, her sparkling demeanour draws her fae friends into a tumult of dance. Fireflies flock to her side, tracing a swirling path of Min Min light all the way from Australia to the Americas.

Akari's dynamism is the prime source of power and excitement in the world. She loves nothing better than to liven up the scene, but she also knows when it's time to turn her energy level down, recharge and let the Moon and Star Fairies take over. Once in a while she falls into a slumber so deep that a sudden, widespread and unexplained power cut will ensue… After all, even fairies need a break sometimes.

Shy Away

If you're feeling a bit shy before a party or event, a simple trick is to create a mantra of confidence. Jot these words down on a slip of paper and shine a light on it. Repeat the mantra three times. Slip the paper into your pocket or purse for a steady beam of courage.

I am confident and sure to have a good time.

NATURE'S GLOW
Certain living things have the ability to glow, either through bioluminescence or biofluorescence. The first is a chemical process that occurs inside a plant, animal, bacteria or fungus. For example, there's a fungus known as foxfire that shines in the woods after sundown. Biofluorescence is another way to glow, this time by absorbing a certain amount of light from another source (such as the Sun) and later releasing it.

SKYLIGHTS
The aurora borealis, also known as the northern lights, is a spectacular celestial light show that has captivated humanity for thousands of years. Energised particles of the Sun smash through the Earth's thin polar atmosphere at high speed, generating mesmerising streaks of bright lights. They appear as curtains of light that seem to dance across the sky. In the southern hemisphere, these polar lights are known as aurora australis.

SPRIGHTLY PUNKS
In British folklore, Hinkypunks and Will o' the Wisps are mischievous creatures that mislead lost travellers by shining their deceptive lights down perilous roads. Hinkypunks live in swampy waters, their ghoulish one-legged form glowing brightly to lure captivated humans. Will o' the Wisps are found in woodlands, taking the form of bright flashes of light that create a falsely reassuring path for those lost in the darkness.

THE STAR FAIRY

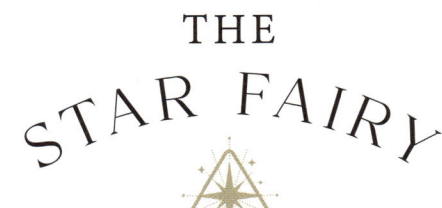

ASTER

The Star Fairies came alive at the first spark of the Big Bang, transforming and radiating warmth and joy across the Universe for billions of years. They have shifted colours, going from blue to red and back again, getting hotter and colder, even growing as big as a giant and then as small as a dwarf. Each of these celestial bodies contains the history of the Universe in their glittering forms.

Led by Aster, the greatest and brightest of their lot, the Star Fairies travel through time and space, illuminating the cosmic web with their sparkling dispositions. They have traced shining maps on the parchment of the sky, allowing travellers throughout history to make their way home – or leading villains astray. Together, they make up a complex constellation of personalities – each reflecting an inimitable mix of spectacular traits and petty flaws – from naughty or nice to utterly neutral. The one feature that these stellar beings share is a meteoric sense of self-love, though their vanity makes them easy prey for the Sea Fairies, who try to pluck them from the sky and drop them into the water to live out the rest of their earthly lives as starfish.

As devoted fans of the Sun Fairy, the Star Fairies aspire to achieve her golden status. They shower her with excessive compliments that massage her already overblown ego. Celebrities in their own right, the Star Fairies are also keen to seduce the Dream Fairy into making their hopes of fame a reality. They are the heroes of their own fantasies, playing out their dramas in lucid reels of cinematic splendour. Following the Neon Fairy's trail, they sneak into concerts to dance wildly in the stage lights with the Poetry and Song Fairies. The youngest of the Star Fairies are the most playful, often darting across the sky in games of hide-and-seek – to the delight of humans watching from below. The most mysterious of all the Star Fairies is the elusive Dark Star Fairy, who has never been seen by anyone besides her siblings.

Sparkling and ethereal, the Star Fairies spend most of their time chatting to each other while reclining on a velvet carpet studded with galactic diamonds. Their glamour never fades but their energy is transformed in a massive explosion to create a new life for themselves. This metamorphosis can sometimes be seen in the sky as a huge burst of light that scientists fondly call a supernova.

Wishing on a Star

On a clear night, go outside and look up at the sky. Select a star that calls to you. Focus on it and make your wish. One of the Star Fairies will be watching over you. Since urban lights cause light pollution, it is easier to see stars in the countryside, but big cities have their bright stars too. Find out more about your chosen star so that you can locate it easily whenever you like. Call it by a name when making your next wish to magnify the magic.

HIGH ENERGY

Stars form when atoms of light elements (such as hydrogen and helium) in a cloud of gas and dust are squeezed by a huge amount of pressure from a nearby explosion, causing their nuclei to get smashed together. This nuclear reaction is called fusion and it produces huge amounts of radiation, which is released as heat and the shining light that has made stars so famous.

STELLAR SPECTRUM

Stars emit light across the entire spectrum, from blue to red. The hottest and brightest stars appear blue, while cooler ones appear red. Our Sun emits white light, although to us it appears yellow. Most stars have enough fuel to shine for several billion years. When a star 'dies', it will explode as a supernova once it has spent all the energy in its core (see more on pages 66–67).

CELESTIAL SKIES

The ancient practice of surveying the constellations has formed the foundation of many belief systems. Many of these cults and religions saw the stars as gods who controlled life on Earth – most importantly, agriculture and hunting. This is manifested in the many names we have for the hunter constellation known as Orion, such as Al-jabbar (the giant) in medieval Muslim astrology or Mriga (deer) in ancient Sanskrit.

LIFE CYCLE OF

The stars of our Universe are scintillating and infinite. With lifetimes of over a billion years, the evolution of these celestial objects is among the most fascinating mysteries in the Cosmos.

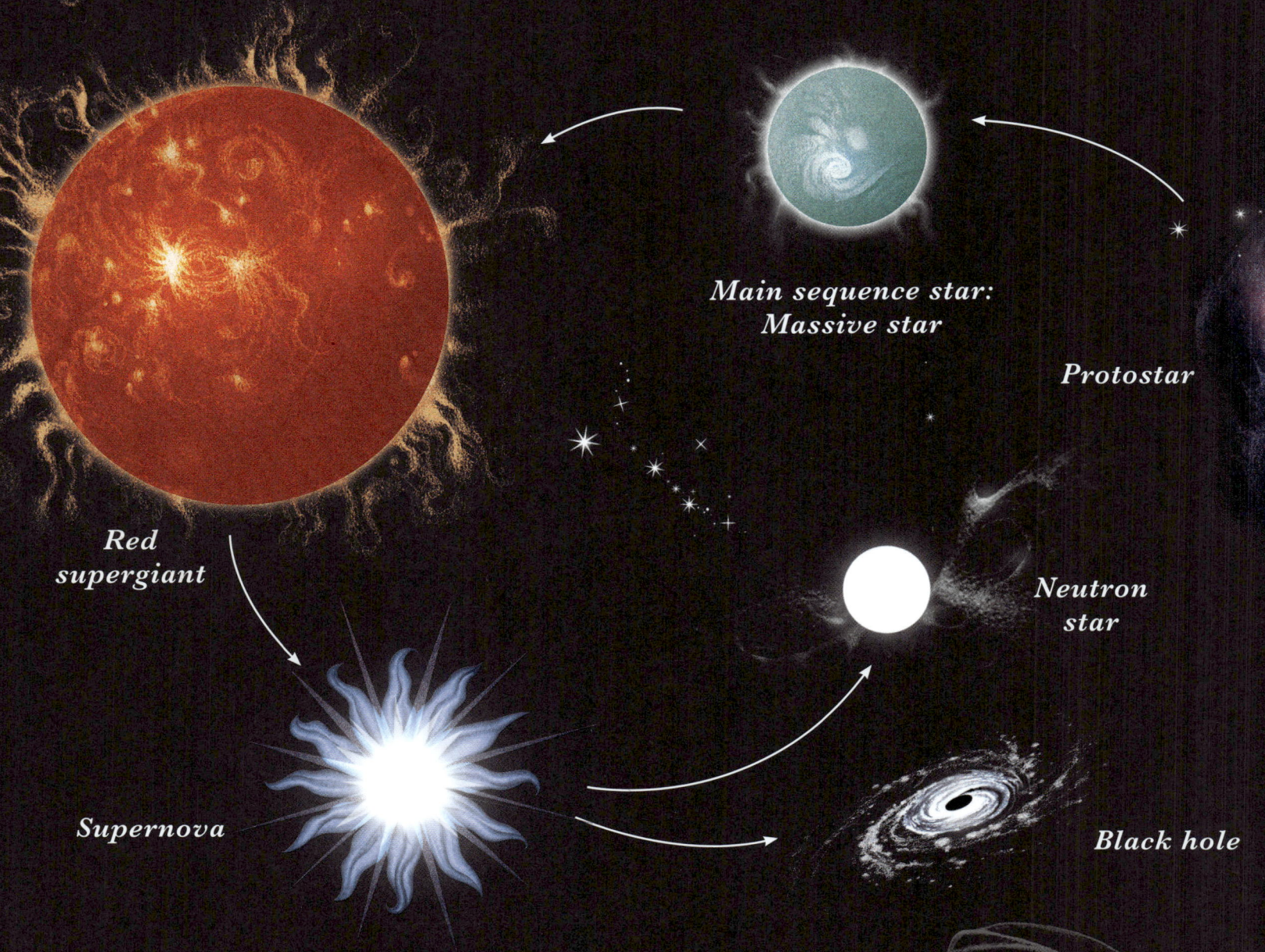

Main sequence star: Massive star

Protostar

Red supergiant

Neutron star

Supernova

Black hole

A STAR IS BORN

All the stars in the Universe are born from the same matter – a cloud of dust and gas called a stellar nebula. The gas is primarily made up of the two lightest elements, hydrogen and helium. Over millions of years, gravity pulls the dust and gas together, squeezing it into a hot ball of gas that is known as a protostar.

As the protostar continues to grow, it gets larger and denser. The bigger it gets, the more dust and gas it continues to attract – until it becomes a massive ball of colliding particles and becomes a fully fledged star.

Interactions among its particles release heat, raising the temperature so high that the nuclei of hydrogen atoms fuse together, creating helium and releasing incredible amounts of energy. This energy keeps the core of the star super hot and makes it shine as energy is released in various forms of radiation such as ultraviolet light, X-rays, visible light, infrared rays, microwaves and radio waves.

UNDER PRESSURE

The huge pressure involved in this process is balanced by the forces of gravity. This balance keeps the star stable for billions of years as it continues to burn the hydrogen fuel stored in its core. A star that has achieved this level of stability is called a main sequence star. Our star, the Sun, the centrepiece of our Solar System, is an example of a main sequence star of average mass. Because of the intense fusion taking place in their cores, massive stars burn through their fuel more quickly. This means they have shorter lifetimes than average stars, but shine much more brightly.

After billions of years of fusion and luminescence, a star will ultimately run out of hydrogen and the fusion reactions stops. Gravity will then take over, pushing the star inwards until it shrinks into a small, very dense ball and the temperature rises again. As a result, nuclear fusion starts up again but this time the star will use the helium it contains to produce heavier elements, such as carbon, oxygen and iron.

A STAR

The Star Fairies are born of these incredible clusters of interstellar dust – just like you, me, everyone and everything in the Universe.

Main sequence star: Average star

Red giant

Planetary nebula

White dwarf

Black dwarf

GIANTS IN THE SKY

At this stage, an average-sized star will form a red giant. Red giants are unstable by nature, and so they eject the outer layer of dust and gas, forming a glowing shell of ionised gas that is called a planetary nebula.

Red giant stars will go on to shrink and form a hot, dense core that is known as a white dwarf. A white dwarf is relatively small and there is no nuclear fusion taking place in its core. It continues to shine brightly until it depletes all its energy, ultimately cooling down and fading into a black dwarf.

A massive star will form a red supergiant. It goes through numerous cycles of expansion and contraction until it finally collapses and explodes in a burst of light known as a supernova. This process leads to the creation of even heavier elements, such as uranium and gold, that are scattered throughout the Universe.

THE NEXT GENERATION

As it cools down, a massive supernova will either condense into a very dense core called a neutron star or it will collapse entirely and form a black hole. Neutron stars don't emit any heat or light; however, they may sometimes be detected thanks to their X-ray emission. A black hole is so dense that its gravity pulls everything into it – even light – which is why it appears invisible. Scientists are still trying to figure out what happens to all the matter and energy that gets sucked into a black hole.

The remnants of extinguished stars end up scattered throughout the Universe, forming new clouds of dust and gas. This leads to the formation of young stellar objects that have the potential to develop into the next generation of stars as the life cycle starts all over again.

AIR FAIRIES

WILHELMINA & GAIL: THE WIND & STORM FAIRIES

LIRAZ: THE VANISHING FAIRY

JAY: THE BIRD FAIRY

SHAYAN & SHA'IRA: THE SONG & POETRY FAIRIES

CELESTE: THE DREAM FAIRY

JAZELLE: THE SHAPESHIFTER FAIRY

Air Fairies

Drawing their power from the life-giving combination of magic and imagination, these evanescent spirits are the inspiration behind the poetry and rhythms of the world. Like the wind, the Air Fairies are changeable, flowing from a breezy complacence to a blustering storm of bravado. When confronted, they will fly off like birds, vanish into a glittering haze or explode in a tornado of emotion. These shifty, unpredictable beings can go from flighty and nebulous to brisk and ferocious in a mere instant. As the original dream weavers, they have the ability to shapeshift and transform reality on a whim. Guardians and messengers between the human world and the mystical realm of the fae, they reveal the hidden truths behind the material tricks of physics.

WILHELMINA & GAIL

THE WIND & STORM FAIRIES

Twin souls born of the same ethereal breeze, the Wind and Storm Fairies couldn't be more different. Despite their opposite personalities, they are a team equipped to face up to any crisis or challenge. Their silhouettes are flimsy and evanescent, but their actions endure for days, months and even ages. Holding dominion over the sky, their realm is eternal, stretching to outer space.

Gail dances gracefully among the newly green leaves of spring, and twirls in the crimson and cadmium foliage of autumn, twisting herself in every direction. Basking in the summer sun, she rustles up the wildflowers in grassy meadows and sprinkles seeds to new destinations. She carries birds, insects and butterflies through the air on her shoulders, gently guiding them across the fields. She wanders coastal regions, whipping up a gentle froth upon the ocean waves and nudging sailboats along their route. She is content in her breezy existence, but often finds herself in the shadow of her more blusterous sibling.

Wilhelmina's power is exponential and intrepid. The branches of the strongest trees sway and crack in her wake. She stirs up the ocean waves and raises them miles into the air, only to suddenly crash them down, smashing everything in sight. Wilhelmina is watchful and wary – even to a fault. When challenged, she flies into an electric rage that whips across the sky in silver flashes of fury. Her voice rumbles through the air in an apocalyptic treble of screams. She is a whirling dervish – the force that drives hurricanes, cyclones, tornadoes, monsoons and typhoons. She carries all the frustration and pain of the world in her heart.

Only Gail can assuage Wilhelmina's wrath. When she hears her sibling's thunderous roar, she swoops in to take her off to a secret lair where she can quell her rage. A pack of shining silver wolves follows on their trail as they rumble across the sky. All that is left of them is the intoxicating scent of wind-whipped rain.

Together, the Wind and Storm Fairies weather every challenge, no matter how catastrophic. Supreme warriors of the sky and heroes of the fairy realm, they offer protection to all the winged creatures both earthly and fae. A mighty duo, they will not hesitate to punish those who threaten their existence.

Gust of Emotion

If you find yourself feeling especially angry or frustrated on a blustery day, find a leaf in a park or garden. With a black marker, draw the symbols of the Wind and Storm Fairies on the leaf. Climb a hill (or even a bench) and toss the leaf into the air. Whisper the following words:

Fairies of the wind and storm, help free me of my fury.

Now watch the leaf swirling in the wind, feeling yourself letting go of your negative emotions as the leaf falls to the ground.

WIND EFFECTS

Wind is the result of the natural movement of air molecules across the Earth's surface, which is compounded by the effect of the planet's rotation (called the Coriolis effect). When cold air (mostly from the poles) clashes with hot air (mostly from around the sunny equator) it creates movement. The hot, high-pressure air moves up and cold, low-pressure wind moves in to replace it, creating gusts of air. The greater the temperature difference between bodies of air, the more intense winds and storms are produced, especially when there is a lot of moisture in the air – leading to extreme weather events like hurricanes and tornadoes.

INTERGALACTIC STORMS

The Sun also has wind, which is a stream of charged particles (mostly electrons and protons) escaping from its surface at speeds of 250–750 kilometres per second! This 'solar wind' is highly radiated and has the potential to cause damage to organic life. Thankfully, the Earth is surrounded by a strong magnetic field that deflects these particles. At the poles, we can see a hint of this solar wind as the aurora borealis since Earth's magnetic field is weaker in these regions. The fastest winds in the Solar System can be found on Neptune (2,000 kilometres per hour) and on Saturn (1,600 kilometres per hour). By comparison, the strongest wind gust ever documented on Earth was recorded on Barrow Island, Australia, in 1996, at 407 kilometres per hour.

NAME GAME

In Irish folklore, there is a fairy called Girle Guairle, whose name translates to 'Stormy Storm'. Her story resembles that of Rumpelstiltskin, with a woman working late into the night spinning and weaving flax thread. Hearing her complaints, the fairy offers to complete her work if she promises to remember her name. In the morning, both thread and fairy are gone. The woman, however, can't remember the fairy's name. Worried, she goes for a walk and comes upon a fairy ring where she hears the fairy boasting of her trick and singing her own name. She returns home and waits for the fairy to return. She is delighted when she can greet her by name after all. Girle Guairle hands over the spinning wheel and disappears in a flurry of rage at being tricked by a human.

AIR
FAIRIES

THE VANISHING FAIRY
LiRAZ

The Vanishing Fairy was born of a luminous spark that spread across the galaxy, stretching the bounds of space-time to the limits of infinity. She is the force that makes the fae kingdom invisible to humans, keeping the portals to this magical realm hidden from sight.

The fairies of Faedom all share the ability to disappear without a trace, but Liraz is the most elusive of all. Her chameleon-like qualities allow her to mesh seamlessly into her surroundings, taking the form of a cloud, a tree or even the waves of the sea. And while she may choose to reveal herself to a curious child wandering through the woods, no adult human has ever managed to spot her, no matter how many devious traps they've set.

As the patron of adventure seekers across the Cosmos, Liraz rewards the dauntless with her mercy and protection. But at the first sign of ill-intent, she will revoke her favour and cast a vanishing spell to confiscate a greedy explorer's fortune.

Fascinated by human trifles and trinkets, she'll pick up any glittering object that takes her fancy. She is even capable of stopping time in its tracks, which can be especially handy when she spies a shiny bit of treasure she desires. Since she is always forgetting to return things to their rightful places, Liraz is the usual suspect when items go missing.

With the power to shrink and expand the fabric of space-time at will, Liraz's vanishing technique is a perfect mix of magic and science. She serves as the chief timekeeper of the fae realm, where the minutes tick by so quickly that a whole decade will pass in a mere earthly minute.

A master of travel, time and transmogrification, Liraz zips through the Universe at the speed of light. Her ethereal silhouette glimmers as she flits between worlds and across dimensions, leaving nothing but a puff of glittering mist in her wake.

Dowsing for Lost Objects

If you ever lose a prized possession, it may be that Liraz has borrowed it and put it in the wrong place. To locate a misplaced item, take a necklace with an amulet or charm attached and hold it steady between your index finger and your thumb. Walk around and if it starts to swirl, it means that you are not far from the object. If Liraz is close, she will use her magic to help you find your lost treasure.

VANISHING TECH

Our vision relies on light reflecting off objects into our eyes, where special cells called photoreceptors convert it to electrical signals. These signals travel to the brain where they are turned into images. Invisibility occurs when light rays refract (bend), distorting the perception of the image. Scientists have been working to adopt this light-bending ability to create invisibility cloaks for humans and objects.

TIME FLEX

On Earth, time is constant and independent of any other forces, such as motion, speed or distance. In the Universe, the passage of time flows differently. Time in outer space is directly related to how fast an object is moving as well as the strength of the gravitational field around it. The faster an object is travelling through space, the greater its potential to 'curve' the fabric of space-time and slow down the passage of time.

GHOSTLY FAE

In British tradition, ashrays (asrai) are translucent fairies who are easily mistaken for ghosts. Native to local lakes and other bodies of water, these fairies only come out at night to bask in the moonlight. Notoriously timid, these enigmatic creatures fear humans. If they are captured or exposed to light or land, they will fade away into a puddle of water.

AIR
FAIRIES

THE BIRD FAIRY

JAY

Swooping through the skies, Jay the Bird Fairy guides all creatures and children who may have been lured off their paths. He protects travellers from the harmful curses of naughty gnomes or wicked wood spirits and leads rescue teams to provide help.

A majestic being, Jay is extremely proud of his splendid looks. He never misses a chance to show off his glorious plumage, spreading his wings so that the indigo feathers shimmer in the light. Their incredible patterns shine with speckles of blue, grey, green and brown in a hypnotising swirl of colour.

Jay is all-seeing, knowing exactly what is happening in both the human and the fae worlds at any time. A professional eavesdropper, he may even turn into a single feather when he wants to listen to a conversation without being spotted. He has accumulated a vast collection of gossip and wisdom, and never misses a chance to reveal what he's learned through the ages. His principal role is to act as a messenger between realms, sharing the secrets of the spirit world with those who want to listen.

Jay also brings news of what humans are scheming so that the fae can prepare, should these actions threaten the integrity of the natural world. His messages are delivered in a unique language that only a special group of code breakers called augurs can interpret. The song of the Bird Fairy is immensely powerful, capable of enchanting anyone who hears it.

A cousin of the Shapeshifter Fairy, he can change form easily, switching from a glorious pheasant to a majestic eagle in an instant. He dances for the Sun Fairy, gracefully dipping and spinning through the air. He bows down to the Rain and Dew Fairy, and casts a broad shadow above the Earth just before the Wind and Storm Fairies join in to take over the skies.

Jay is also tasked with spreading forgiveness. He helps those who grapple with a guilty conscience to atone for their wrongdoing, freeing them from remorse. A vulnerable creature in his own right, Jay's ego is easily bruised. When his temper flares, he'll burst forth in a thunderous bout of beating wings and furious squawks.

Feather of Atonement

Try invoking the power of Jay with this ritual. Find a feather on the ground, pick it up and rinse it in warm water. Leave it to dry and wash your hands. Then, decorate it by dipping it in paint. On a small piece of paper write down what you would like to apologise for, roll it into a tube, fasten it with a piece of string or ribbon and tie it to the feather. Hold the note and swirl the feather around, chanting:

Jay, master of forgiveness, give me the courage to apologise for my mistake.

BIRD BALLET
Many species of bird have evolved elaborate plumage and courtship rituals to attract potential partners. Each species perfects the moves of its own special dance, complete with spins, graceful flicks of the feathers and startling sound effects. The most spectacular show is put on by the birds of paradise of New Guinea, with plumage and poses that rival those of the most accomplished prima ballerinas. The more elaborate the dance, the better the bird's chances of winning the attention of a mate.

MAGICAL MIMICRY
Australian ground-dwelling birds known as lyrebirds are some of the most convincing mimics of the animal world, capable of imitating the sounds of dogs barking, music playing, people speaking and even children crying. They can recreate most sounds they hear. This ability is attributed to an organ in their throat called the syrinx which is very highly developed in these particular species.

NATIVE THUNDER
The thunderbird is a powerful myth shared by many Native American tribes, particularly among Algonquian and Siouan-speaking peoples. Enormous and colourful with strong talons, it resides in the clouds above the highest mountain peaks. The flapping of its wings creates thunder and lightning comes from its flashing eyes, and it brings rain to arid areas to encourage crops to grow. When angered, the thunderbird might even cause storms, floods or fire.

AIR
FAIRIES

SHAYAN & SHA'IRA

THE SONG & POETRY FAIRIES

Shayan and Sha'ira are an inseparable pair, an ancient fairy couple dating back to when the first notions of human language and civilisation began to take shape. They are the original muses of the greatest stories ever told, experts at harnessing the power of lyricism, which is the source of all magic in the world.

Together, Shayan and Sha'ira compose the symphonic hum of the Universe from the moment of its birth – the cymbals and strings of the Big Bang – to the present day. From tragedies to comedies, they are the ones tugging at your heartstrings when you hear a certain verse or refrain that captures your imagination.

Their incantations and spells make the Sun shine, rain fall and plants grow according to the natural rhythm that rules the Cosmos. At times, they may bicker and fall out of rhythm, creating discordant melodies that carry a chaotic power to enchant and bewitch, giving life to exciting new genres and novel instruments.

Together with their fae friend the Neon Fairy, they are always at the head of the ceremonial rades held on the high holidays of the fae calendar. They lead a trooping cavalcade of mystical beings and beasts on their pipes, flutes, fiddles, trumpets and bells, chanting and trilling through the villages, towns and cities of the world. This mysterious chorus weaves its way to a secret glade among the trees that marks the sacred location of the fairy feast. Here the fae folk assemble into a circle of revelry and begin to sing, dance and play music with utter abandon.

Shayan and Sha'ira have given humanity a generous gift that cannot always be seen, but is heard and felt by all. Their inspiration has been the very breath of existence since the beginning of time. Their songs are carried on the wind, their lyrics fluttering in the trees.

On the rare occasion that a human being might intrude upon these magical celebrations, a sip of nectar and a soothing song will lull them into a deep sleep filled with enchanted dreams.

ANCIENT SONGS

The word 'poetry' comes from the Greek word *poieo*, meaning 'I create'. The first poems were typically chanted or sung as a way of passing down history before writing was invented. The oldest recorded poem is the *Epic of Gilgamesh*, set down in stone in ancient Mesopotamia (modern-day Iraq) around 4,000 years ago. In Ancient Greece, poetry flourished in the epic works of Homer and in the lyricism of Sappho. Scholars recently uncovered a narrative poem on a clay tablet attributed to the high priestess Enheduanna in ancient Mesopotamia, more than 4,000 years ago. The ancient Sanskrit word for music is *sangeet*, which literally means 'sung together', whereas in most European languages, 'music' comes from the Greek word 'mousike'.

SOUND BATHING

This technique uses a singing bowl to create resonant vibrations that are said to soothe the mind and body. This tradition comes from Nepal and India, dating back 5,000 years. This method can induce a meditative and sleepy state that has been widely adopted to decrease stress and anxiety. Indeed, scientists have confirmed that the effect of music on the brain leads to the release of 'happy hormones' like dopamine and serotonin.

SIREN CALL

Fairy lore is full of musical fae, such as Scotland's loireag, who punish those who sing out of tune, Sweden's näcken, who are the strictest of violin instructors, and the Cherokee Yunwi Tsunsdi, whose drumming reverberates through the forests and mountains of Appalachia. In Greek mythology, Ulysses had to be bound to his ship's mast to escape the enticing call of the Sirens.

Rhymes and Chimes

To make your own wind chime, first find a flexible twig that you can bend and use for your base. Gather another seven thick twigs and paint and decorate them as you like. Tie each one to the end of a string, along with stones, shells, beads or sea glass, and hang these on your base. When ready, hang your wind chime wherever you want, in the garden or indoors.

Chant the following message to the fairies:

Shayan and Sha'ira, fairies of inspiration, help me create a beautiful composition.

AIR FAIRIES

THE DREAM FAIRY

CELESTE

Drifting on the cusp of fantasy and reality, the Dream Fairy travels between dimensions. A skilled dream-maker, she weaves together a magical mix of colours, tailoring settings, landscapes and characters. She raises the power of imagination to bewildering heights.

Celeste is known to inspire artists, philosophers and inventors to come up with novel ideas, stories and solutions to problems. Her wondrous reveries will alleviate boredom – although she may unwittingly cause pesky bouts of absent-mindedness and forgetfulness. Her extraordinary power means she can glimpse into the future. Sometimes she shares her visions with dreamers in the form of cryptic scenes or symbols that only the most astute can interpret.

She is the fiercest guardian of her intangible realm. She protects dreamers from malicious interlopers who try to slip through her celestial portal with the intention to incite fear and dim the bright lights of the dreamworld. Ready to face any such monster, she launches magical arrows to subdue and trap these enemies, before locking them in a mystical bubble of glass and banishing them to the hellish realm they escaped from.

The Dream Fairy is often accompanied by Yumi, a white dove. When a nightmare becomes too tarrying, Celeste sends Yumi to pick up the slumbering spirit of the dreamer and drop them back into reality, waking the anguished sleeper so abruptly that they will experience a sudden sensation of falling through the sky.

When bedtime approaches, this gentle fairy will summon some of her dearest fae friends to create a balmy symphony of sensory delights. The Moon Fairy lends her soft, comforting light, while the Rain and Dew Fairy taps out a tinkling melody. The Song and Poetry Fairies whisper the most captivating tales to draw a sleepy subject into dreamland. As their charms take over, Celeste will sprinkle a pinch of stardust into the air to promote a deep, dreamful slumber.

Lucid Dreaming

One of the most helpful tools for banishing nightmares is something known as 'lucid dreaming'. This is when you are still asleep but remain aware of the fact that you are dreaming. With practice, dreamers can learn to control the dream narrative and create a world where everything is possible or even return to the same dream setting. If there is a dream you would like the Dream Fairy to help you create, write out the scene in a special journal.

STUFF OF DREAMS

Even if we can't remember our dreams, science has shown that our brains actively come up with images and ideas when we are asleep. Interestingly, our longest dreams usually come to us in the morning. The stage of sleep when we typically dream is called REM. This stage is also when the front part of our brain that controls how we make sense of things is deactivated. This is why our dreams can often feel quite realistic.

ANCESTRAL OMENS

Many folk traditions assign meanings to dreams as a space for communication between human and the divine or the ancestral plane. The Bantu people of Africa believe that messages from their ancestors are passed down through dreams. These messages are interpreted as good omens or warnings for the future. Take a look at some of the symbols that dream interpreters use to decipher our dreams (on the right).

DREAMY DIVINATION

Some key symbols in dream interpretation:

Chase: Fear of an impending challenge.
Cat: Anticipation of an unexpected event.
Getting lost: Alienation from our surroundings or loved ones.
Rainbow: Feeling hopeful about an optimistic turn of events up ahead.
Teeth falling out: Anxiety about an impending change or major life event.

THE SHAPESHIFTER FAIRY
JAZELLE

Fairies are famous for their beguiling ways and their shapeshifting abilities. But only the most ancient and accomplished have perfected the ability to shapeshift at will. Jazelle is the supreme mistress of visual deception and optical illusion.

Whatever form Jazelle takes on at dawn is the creature or persona she will embody for twenty-four hours, and her shapeshifting is governed by her mood. She will go from a happy-go-lucky dove to a powerful panther or slinky reptile overnight. She can shrink to a small hummingbird or expand into an elephant. When she is feeling especially powerful, she will become a unicorn or even a fire-breathing dragon. Yet her favourite incarnation is that of a crafty and comely fox.

A proud fairy, Jazelle shapeshifts in secret, and only when her metamorphosis is complete does she emerge, ready to face the day. Sometimes she does it for fun, often mischievously playing tricks on her fellow fairies, impersonating them or interfering with their duties. She will burn the Kitchen Fairy's pies and taunt the Mouse Fairy by turning into a cat.

Jazelle's thirst for experiences is boundless. She yearns to soar through the skies like an eagle, to swim through the seas like a dolphin and prowl the forest like a fox. A natural-born trickster, she enjoys astonishing audiences with her transformative powers. When she feels especially huffy, she may simply embody the wind and appear to vanish in a single sparkling puff, though she has not yet acquired the magic of the Vanishing Fairy to disappear entirely.

Despite her impish tendencies, Jazelle is cherished by her friends because there is no ill will in her mischief. She just simply cannot help herself. She does her best to make up for any insensitive jest by turning herself into a little kitten and quenching any anger with an absurd serving of cuteness.

The most compelling lesson of the Shapeshifting Fairy is that we can never trust our eyes completely, but intuition can help us to uncover the hidden truths of reality.

Blending-in Beads

If there is an event coming up and you are worried that you might not fit in, make this magical beaded bracelet to channel some of Jazelle's shapeshifting, adaptive power. You will need string, some beads with letters on them and any other decorative beads or charms you wish to use. Arrange the patterns as you wish and spell out the name Jazelle with your beads (or just the letter J). Leave it on the windowsill so that Jazelle can charge it with some of her feisty spirit.

NATURAL MAGIC

Some animals are known to shapeshift. This process is called metamorphosis and butterflies are the most accomplished practitioners of this incredible natural magic. Once a special hormone is released, the dormant 'butterfly cells' in a caterpillar's body begin to multiply, becoming a chrysalis. The cells of the caterpillar are 'recycled' to build the wings and all the other body parts and systems required for a mature butterfly.

SNEAKY CREATURES

The mimic octopus has the ingenious ability to impersonate a range of creatures to escape from predators. It can imitate the shape and colouring of a deadly lionfish or tuck in six of its arms to resemble an equally venomous banded sea snake. The immortal jellyfish can transform back into an immature polyp at the first sign of danger and regrow a whole new generation of jellyfish genetically identical to the original one.

FOXY FIGURES

In Korean tradition, there is a shapeshifting fox spirit called a kumiho, akin to the kitsune of Japan and the huli jing of China. The kumiho is an ancient fox who has prowled the Earth for at least 1,000 years and gained the ability to transform into a human with fox-like features. Stories tell of a kumiho who took on a womanly form to find a husband, but the nuptials sparked a curse that tormented the newlyweds thereafter.

AIR FAIRIES

EARTH

Rowan: The Tree Fairy
Stands tall in the world's most ancient woods, such as the Sherwood Forest in England, Taman Negara Rainforest in Malaysia and Mau Forest of Kenya.

Rosie, Peony & Azalea: The Flower Fairies
Nestled in the lavender fields of Luberon in France, rare orchids of Puerto Vallarta in Mexico, lotus blossoms of the Humble Administrator's Garden in China and the rosebushes of Butchart Gardens in Canada.

Esmeralda: The Moss & Meadow Fairy
Seen descending the emerald terraces of the Sapa Valley in Vietnam, hiking through Teahupo'o in Tahiti and MacGillycuddy's Reeks in Ireland, or strolling the lush hills of Moti Korval in India.

Niah: The Cave Fairy
Known to dwell in the secretive depths of the world's most spectacular caves, such as the Caves of Hercules in Morocco, Škocjan Caves in Slovenia, Hang Sơn Đoòng in Vietnam and the Waitomo Glowworm Caves of New Zealand. She also enjoys a splash in the underground pools of the Crystal Caves in Bermuda.

Sorella: The Mouse Fairy
Found scampering through all the country fields and cities of the globe, from the great plains of Saskatchewan in Canada and the pampas of South America to the savannahs of Botswana.

Lunella: The Moon Fairy
Shines her brightest during the Lunar New Year celebrations in Beijing and Hong Kong, and dazzles over the lookout point at Mount Chimborazo in Ecuador, the Earth's closest location to the Moon.

WATER

Marina: The Oceans & Seas Fairy
See her swimming along the main currents from north to south and east to west across the seven seas, lingering among the turquoise waters of the Azores, the lush islands of Hawai'i and the archipelagos of Indonesia.

Nephelie: The Mist & Steam Fairy
As a fan of the city, she is drawn to the bustle of New York City and Paris as well as the manufacturing hubs of Guangzhou and Tianjin in China. She takes breaks in the thermal pools of Pamukkale in Turkey and Banjar in Indonesia.

Ondine: The Rivers & Lakes Fairy
Dwells in the lochs of Awe and Morar in Scotland and Geirangerfjord in Norway. She may surf with pink river dolphins on the Amazon and skip stones across Lake Titicaca in South America and Lake Baikal in Siberia.

Isa: The Snow & Ice Fairy
At home in the most frigid and isolated places on Earth, such as Dome Fuji in Antarctica, North Ice in Greenland and Denali, Alaska.

Talia: The Rain & Dew Fairy
Enjoys orchestrating symphonies of rain and hail across Debundscha in Cameroon, Cobija in Bolivia and the East Khasi Hills of India.

Skylar: The Rainbow Fairy
Dances among the most dazzling waterfalls from Iguazu Falls of Argentina and Brazil to Blue Nile Falls of Ethiopia and Kahiwa Falls of Hawai'i.

FIRE

Solange: The Sun Fairy
Basks in the heat of the most radiant locales, including Toliara in Madagascar, Belle Mare in Mauritius and Yuma in Arizona, the sunniest spot on Earth.

Seraphina: The Lava Fairy
Erupts across the most volatile volcanic regions, including Mount Nyiragongo in the Democratic Republic of the Congo, Mount Semeru in Indonesia, Mount Etna in Sicily and Iceland's famous Eyjafjallajökull.

Farah: The Desert Fairy
Thrives in the scorching sands of the Sahara in North Africa, the Gobi in northern China and southern Mongolia and other deserts, finding sanctuary in storytelling over tea in their rare oases.

Alma: The Kitchen Fairy
Right at home wherever there is a hearty stew boiling on the stove. She is drawn in by the fragrant cuisines rising into the skies above Guadeloupe in the Caribbean, Asmara in Eritrea, Kashmir in India and Krabi in Thailand.

Akari: The Neon Fairy
Revels in the lights and noise of Naples, Hong Kong, Tokyo and Dubai. She can also be seen fluttering in the Min Min lights of Australia and the aurora borealis above Tromsø in Norway.

Aster: The Star Fairy
Inhabits the Dark Sky Parks in New Mexico, Atacama Desert, Pic du Midi in France and Ngorongoro Crater in Tanzania.

AIR

Wilhelmina & Gail: The Wind & Storm Fairies
Tend to wreak havoc in the skies close to the equator, stirring up thunder and lightning in tropical locales such as Zulia in Venezuela, Markansu Desert in Tajikistan, Java in Indonesia and Artemisa in Cuba.

Liraz: The Vanishing Fairy
Everywhere and nowhere at once, as the most impossible of the fae to seek out. She can make herself known in other ways, such as a gentle touch on the shoulder when someone is especially lost in thought.

Jay: The Bird Fairy
Blazes his trail along the ancient migratory trails in the skies above all seven continents. He can also be spotted taking a breather on the islands of Montserrat, Aruba, Trinidad and Tobago in the Caribbean or Eighty Mile Beach in Australia.

Shayan & Sha'ira: The Song & Poetry Fairies
Spot them on concert stages and music festivals everywhere, including Coachella in California, Glastonbury in England, Tomorrowland in Belgium, Mawazine in Rabat, Morocco and Sunburn in Goa, India.

Celeste: The Dream Fairy
Like her vanishing sister, she has rarely been spotted outside of the realm of dreams and imagination. She may pay a visit to those who wish to see her as soon as they have passed into the threshold of deep sleep.

Jazelle: The Shapeshifter Fairy
Eludes everyone the moment she is seen, switching seamlessly from a common (albeit cunning) red fox to the 'punk rock' rain frog of the Andes – and every other incarnation you might possibly imagine.

KEY

Reports of fairy sightings have trickled in from all over the world throughout the centuries. Here are some of the most likely places the fae might be spotted. How far would you travel to find a fairy?

- Rowan: The Tree Fairy
- Rosie, Peony & Azalea: The Flower Fairies
- Esmeralda: The Moss & Meadow Fairy
- Niah: The Cave Fairy
- Sorella: The Mouse Fairy
- Lunella: The Moon Fairy

FEASTS & FAE DAYS

The fae calendar is packed with feasts and festivities that celebrate the marvels of nature and the novelties of each new season. Since ancient times, these celebrations have provided an opportunity for the human and the fae realms to unite, as the portals between them open up for a sliver in time. During these rare windows, the veil between these worlds is most tenuous and quite easily crossed. Fairies embark on a massive cavalcade of song and dance, marching through the magical bridges and portals that unite Faedom and Earth in a boisterous, melodic throng. In their revelry, the fae let down their guard, making them more susceptible to being spotted by humans. On rare occasions, a human might be welcome to take part in a fairy rade, but they must take care not to indulge too deeply in these festivities and under no circumstances should they consume even the tiniest morsel of fairy food. Otherwise, they might fall into Faedom and face the arduous challenge of getting back to their terrestrial home.

---

12 JANUARY
Sorella: The Mouse Fairy
All month long, this fairy burrows indoors, collecting as many milk teeth as she can find in return for double the trinkets and coins.

26 JANUARY
Celeste: The Dream Fairy
At a time when the most fanciful and meaningful dreams come about, make sure to get plenty of sleep. Start a new dream journal perhaps.

1–2 FEBRUARY
LUMINA FESTIVAL
(Southern Hemisphere: 1–2 August)
This celebration regales in the gradual return of light in the final weeks of winter. Fire Fairies gather in celebration, glowing bright as they gradually chase the winter away to welcome in the spring. The Flower Fairies get to work, reviving the soil with the first hint of green grass and a peek of snowdrops and crocuses.

13 FEBRUARY
Niah: The Cave Fairy
It's time to shine. Bring out all the gems, jewels and treasures for a spectacular costume party or masked ball with family and friends.

29 FEBRUARY
Liraz: The Vanishing Fairy
This is the perfect opportunity to keep an eye out for lost objects, as Liraz leaps through the world to return many of the items she has 'borrowed' over the year.

5 MARCH
Rowan: The Tree Fairy
Let yourself be drawn to a particular tree in a local garden or park. Take a moment to lean in and absorb some of its deep-rooted magic.

20–23 MARCH
HARMONY FESTIVAL
(Southern Hemisphere: 21–24 September)
It is the first day of spring and a rare moment when day and night share equal portions of the day. The Earth Fairies wake the hibernating world of the north and paint it with a fresh coat of green leaves and flowers of every hue. As a celebration of the start of nature's revival, this is a time of incredible energy.

23 MARCH
Esmeralda: The Moss & Meadow Fairy
Seek out the first glimpses of green as spring prepares to burst forth in bloom. Plant your own seeds around this day in a pot with a wish. They will grow strong and resplendent.

1 APRIL
Jay: The Bird Fairy
Tell jokes and play pranks on this trickster's holiday. You could also help our feathered friends to build new nests by leaving some small, supple twigs or piles of leaves outside.

22 APRIL
Talia: The Rain & Dew Fairy
Indulge in a rain dance at the first spring shower, or you could collect a pot of raindrops for watering any young seedlings you've recently planted.

30 APRIL–1 MAY
BLOOM FESTIVAL
(Southern Hemisphere 1 November)
This is probably the busiest month in all the fae calendar, with endless parties and rades. This feast is honoured with a grand procession of light, colour, music, dancing, friendship and joy. Indulge in rituals that are dedicated to beauty, love, renewal and rejuvenation.

8 MAY
Seraphina: The Lava Fairy
Embrace the natural warmth of the world and take this opportunity to confide in others. Seraphina is a keen believer that a problem shared is a problem halved.

24 MAY
Shayan & Sha'ira: The Song & Poetry Fairies
This is the ideal time to let inspiration take over and dive into your imagination. Think about creating your own poem, song or story.

9 JUNE
Rosie, Peony & Azalea: The Flower Fairies
Seek out the flowering wildflowers and make a fae crown or daisy chain. Or, if you prefer, you can use tissue paper to make a colourful garland.

19–23 JUNE
FLAME FESTIVAL
(Southern Hemisphere: 19–23 December)
On the longest day of the year, the Sun Fairy regains her shining glory for a midsummer feast in her honour. This is a wondrous time when fairies may linger in the human world. It is also a time of forgiveness, when fairies bury the hatchet and wipe the slate clean so that they may all enjoy the fruits of the season together.

28 JUNE
Skylar: The Rainbow Fairy
Keep a lookout for rainbows in the sky and all over town as the glory of summer takes over. Wear bright colours and even celebrate with a rainbow cake to manifest joy and positivity.

6 JULY
Solange: The Sun Fairy
In the northern hemisphere, plan a picnic with plenty of friends to make the most of the Sun's life-giving light. In the southern hemisphere, wear bright colours and think sunny thoughts.

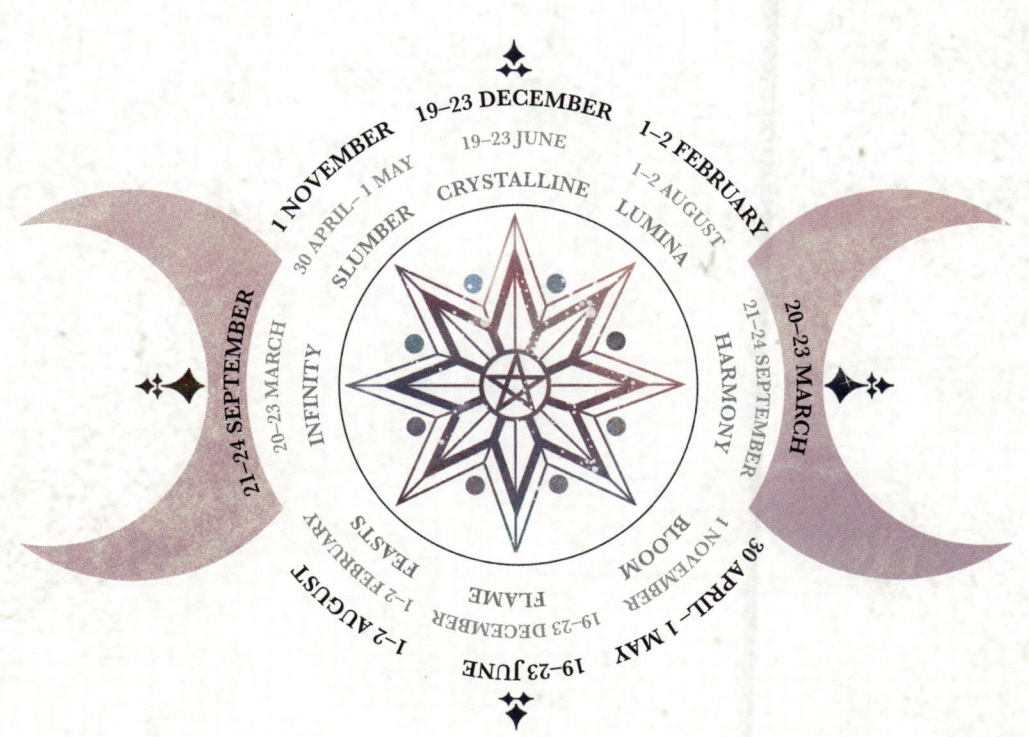

30 JULY
Marina: The Sea Fairy
This is the best time for a seaside celebration. Frolic in the waves, seek out treasures in tidal pools and spell out your wishes in the sand.

1–2 AUGUST
FESTIVAL OF FEASTS
(Southern Hemisphere: 1–2 February)
Time to celebrate the first harvest of the year and share its bounties with family, friends and neighbours. The Kitchen Fairy is particularly busy around this time, travelling the world to collect herbs, spices, fruits, vegetables and grains. She puts on a lavish banquet to share with humans and fae, before supervising the preparation of the soil just before springtime begins in the opposite hemisphere.

16 AUGUST
Farah: The Desert Fairy
Seek shelter from the scorching heat by creating your own oasis in a tent filled with cushions, plants and plenty of refreshing fruit-sprigged iced tea.

27 AUGUST
Jazelle: The Shapeshifter Fairy
Now that summer is in full swing, keep watch for all the different forms Liraz may take on to pay you a visit. She could appear as a fluttering butterfly or a cardinal spider creeping across the ceiling.

2 SEPTEMBER
Ondine: The Rivers & Lakes Fairy
Let yourself go with the flow like a rushing river and be open to all the new possibilities that lie ahead.

21–24 SEPTEMBER
INFINITY FESTIVAL
(Southern Hemisphere: 20-23 March)
During this gloriously cosy season, the night will dominate the skies. Just before conceding defeat, day responds in a burst of golden light, as all of Earth's green turns crimson and orange. These magnificent colours trace a path for the Moon Fairy to follow.

25 SEPTEMBER
Lunella: The Moon Fairy
Stay up a bit later to focus on your secret hopes and dreams around the time of the full moon. Use your sharpened senses to explore your future goals.

3 OCTOBER
Wilhelmina & Gail:
The Wind & Storm Fairies
Celebrate the spooky season with a storytelling circle of ghostly tales and sip warm cups of hot chocolate as the wind whispers through the trees.

18 OCTOBER
Nephelie: The Mist & Steam Fairy
As the days grow colder, let the hisses and pings of steam power you up and give you energy for ingenuity and creativity, even on the cloudiest days.

1 NOVEMBER
SLUMBER FESTIVAL
(Southern Hemisphere: 30 April–1 May)
This festival marks the end of the light season and embraces the dark season of encroaching winter. Nature prepares itself for a time of rest, with animals making burrows and nests in time for hibernation. On the eve of this day, fairies and humans pay tribute to those who are on the other side and ask for their wisdom in making important decisions.

4 NOVEMBER
Akari: The Neon Fairy
Light up the darkness with a late-night dance party, or look out for fireworks and light shows.

20 NOVEMBER
Alma: The Kitchen Fairy
Honour the harvest by lending a hand to prepare hearty meals and scrumptious pies this month. Express your gratitude for the Earth's bounty with a festive meal with loved ones.

7 DECEMBER
Aster: The Star Fairy
Make a wish upon one of the seven most intensely sparkling Pleiades: Electra, Taygete, Maia, Celaeno, Alcyone, Sterope and Merope!

10 DECEMBER
Isa: The Snow & Ice Fairy
If you're in a snowy location, indulge in a snowball fight with friends. If you're in the south, make your own ice lollies or repurpose plasticine moulds to create mini ice sculptures.

19–23 DECEMBER
CRYSTALLINE FESTIVAL
(Southern Hemisphere: 19–23 June)
The merriest of all the feasts, when the fae illuminate the world with light and song. The Snow and Ice Fairy fills glacial landscapes with blankets of snow, frost and ice. She gathers her fellow fae around pines and mistletoe to enjoy hot chocolate, cinnamon buns and fruitcake on the longest night of the year. This is a time for making wishes and forging new beginnings.

FAEOLOGY

Each of the fae reveal a unique mix of attributes, talents, quirks, tendencies and flaws. Their personalities flow between the ethereal, majestic, poised and sanguine, to tricky, moody, boisterous and impetuous.

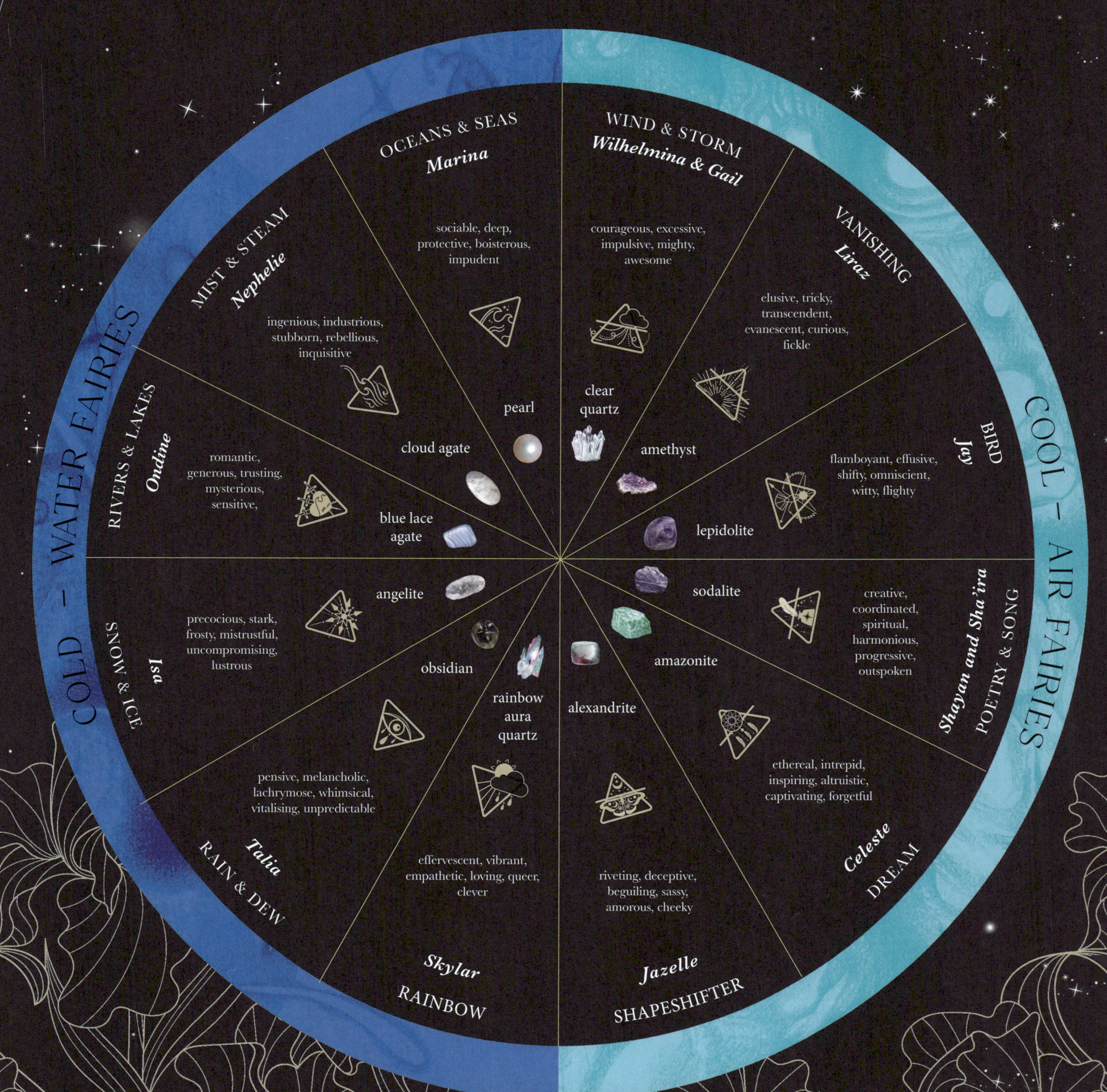

CHARTS

There is a glimmer of fae in each of us.
Which of the fae is most like you?

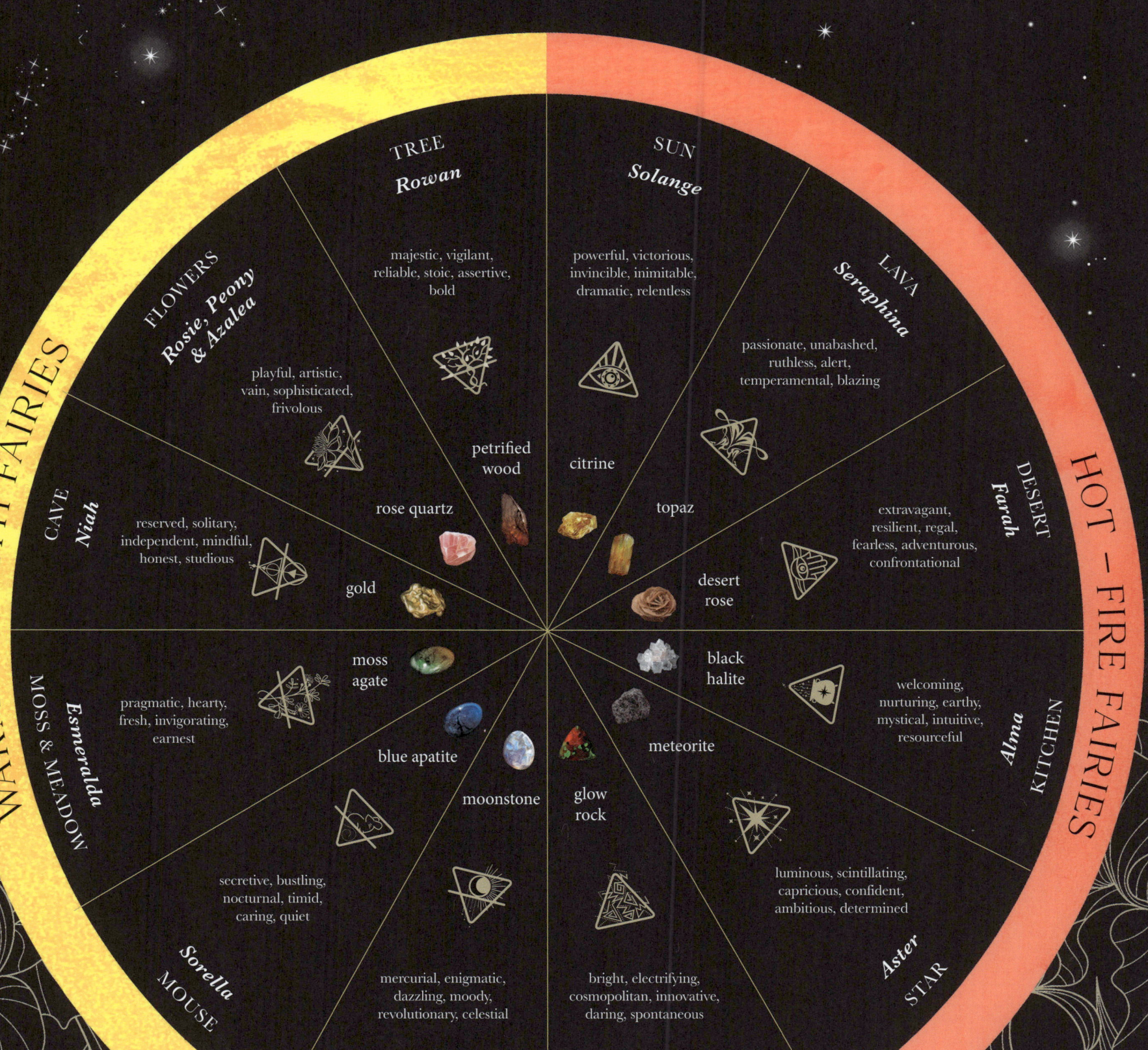

AGNES MONOD-GAYRAUD IS A WRITER AND TRANSLATOR SPECIALISING IN FICTION AND NON-FICTION BOOKS THAT MERGE ELEMENTS OF SCIENCE, NATURE, ART AND FOLKLORE. SHE ALSO WORKS AS A LANGUAGE EDITOR AT THE ASTRONOMY & ASTROPHYSICS JOURNAL. A NATIVE NEW YORKER, SHE IS NOW BASED IN LONDON.

LORNA WHITE IS A WRITER WHO IS FASCINATED BY ALL THINGS MYSTICAL AND MAGICAL. SHE DRAWS HER INSPIRATION FROM EUROPEAN FOLKLORE, FAIRY TALES AND GREEK AND ROMAN MYTHS. HALF-FRENCH, HALF-ENGLISH, SHE GREW UP FLITTING BETWEEN THE TWO NATIONS. SHE CURRENTLY LIVES IN LONDON WITH HER HUSBAND AND TWO DAUGHTERS.

NADZEYA MAKEYEVA IS IS AN OBJECTIVE ARTIST AND ILLUSTRATOR FROM BELARUS, LIVING AND WORKING IN SAN FRANCISCO. SHE'S A MEMBER OF THE SOCIETY OF ILLUSTRATORS OF LOS ANGELES, THE BELARUSIAN UNION OF DESIGNERS AND ARTSPAN'S SAN FRANCISCO ARTIST COMMUNITY.